CONFESSIONS

OF A

Private
Tutor

CONFESSIONS
OF A
Private
Tutor

VIKRAM MATHUR

RUPA

Published by
Rupa Publications India Pvt. Ltd 2013
7/16, Ansari Road, Daryaganj
New Delhi 110002

Sales centres:
Allahabad Bengaluru Chennai
Hyderabad Jaipur Kathmandu
Kolkata Mumbai

ISBN: 978-81-291-2394-7

10 9 8 7 6 5 4 3 2 1

Typeset in Adobe Garamond 12/16 by Jojy Philip, New Delhi.

Printed at Thomson Press India Ltd, Faridabad.

To Amrita

For something that ended so badly, it began without fanfare, in a house with a view of the Arabian Sea.

The boy I was supposed to teach was a spoilt brat, but I was used to that. As long as they weren't rude to me, I didn't care. I didn't even particularly care if they grew to like mathematics. I just wanted them to pass. If they did better—such is the nature of the beast—they got addicted to success and, without knowing it, without even wanting to, they began to work harder. If they didn't do better at mathematics, I got sacked, but there was always a waiting list of students and another kid and another home and another way of making tea.

Pralay Jha was not doing well and his mother asked, through one of his elder sisters, if we could have a conference.

I should have suspected trouble the moment she used the word 'conference'. Most parents would just come into the room in the middle of the lesson and park their butts in another chair and ask you why their sons and heirs (or daughters and chattels) were not doing well. To which, the time-honoured response works well enough: 'S/he could do much better, but s/he must decide that s/he wants to.'

This one wanted a conference. Perhaps it was just the sister's word. She had probably heard it in an American film and wanted to use it.

'We cannot talk in the middle of this chaos,' said Mrs Jha. Chaos? We were sitting in a room large enough to take in my entire home. There were two of us here, while at home there were always at least two people in my field of vision. To me this was the peace and quiet of an oasis in the desert, but I held my tongue. 'I'll take you to coffee at the Taj.'

The Taj? Wow. I had never been taken to the Taj, only walked through it a couple of times when my parents had taken us to see our relatives in Colaba.

'Wear a nice shirt,' she said and threw me a smile over her shoulder. It was the kind of smile that said: 'You have been looking at my body'.

I had not. I swear I had not. Most of the kids I taught were pretty fucked up. Their parents were absent or cold or unforgiving, sometimes all of the above. I could see how these kids worked hard for love, how they were broken by the conditions that were placed upon the receiving of it, how they went from perfectly ordinary children to monsters and then were blamed for it. I didn't want to contribute to their fucked-up-ness, so I left my libido with my shoes at the door.

This is not as difficult as it seems, except when you meet a flirtatious young fifteen-year-old... But I'm getting ahead of myself. Let's just start at the very beginning, the very best place to start, as Maria soon-to-be-von-Trapp sang.

I didn't have too many good shirts. Just two. One was for parties with friends and the other was for this kind of event, the date, the social outing. I was aware, even as I put it on, that it was now about three years old and that it had begun to look a little tired. The patches under the arms were rough and the last button had been replaced by one of my sisters with a button of another colour. But at least the body underneath it was in good shape. We didn't bother about six-packs then; we thought about shoulders and arms. My shoulders were good, my arms bulged. Vincy, my gym sir, had said once: 'Pay attention to your triceps, and your biceps will look after themselves.' It was good advice. For some reason, your triceps work better at swelling out the sleeve of your shirt than your biceps. Perhaps it's because your arm is at rest against your side more often than your elbow is bent up against your upper arm. And I knew that my calves and thighs were fit to be seen. All that walking, from home to home, up the slope of Pedder Road, down the slant of Malabar Hill, up the steps, down the steps. Every day, I logged several kilometres in the Millionaire Mile between Mahalaxmi Temple at one end and Walkeshwar at the other. The distances were too short for taxis to be willing to come; the wait for buses was too long. Yes, my legs were in good shape. You couldn't bounce a coin off my glutes, but why would you want to?

I arrived at the Jha home at 11 a.m., as instructed.

'Would you care to go out?' Mrs Jha asked. 'Or we could stay at home and be comfortable.'

I was so raw, I didn't even think this one through.

'You did say coffee at the Taj?' I said.

She looked at me for one long moment and then said, 'Then coffee at the Taj it shall be.' She smiled, once again with a glint of mischief. 'I try not to disappoint.'

'I'm sure you don't,' I said, which was a foolish thing to say. Nothing much as a comeback, but it was the best I could do at that point because I was looking at her with new eyes.

I didn't know much about her. I knew her name was Prema and that she had been widowed several years ago. She had two daughters, both gorgeous, both very different from each other and from her. I had studiously avoided looking at these two young women, although they often sauntered through the room, leaving it full of rich woman smells.

I should say that Pralay was a late joinee. I inherited him from Pandey Sir, who had shifted his base to the north of Mumbai after retiring from a school in the Millionaire Mile. I paid him a thousand rupees for the referral, but the only time I could make for Pralay was at seven-thirty in the morning. He would be up and ready in his school whites, but the college-going elder sisters would be just drifting into the dining room where we were studying, ripe with sleep. I remember a moment when one of them took a long, deep angdaai, and her beautiful breasts pushed up against the chenille of her nightgown. (Was it chenille?) It was the next morning when I used the image while I was masturbating as I soaped myself during my bath. That self-pleasing quickie was the highlight of my day; it helped me keep my libido in check and it kept me in touch with my sexual self. For the rest of the day, my penis lay inside my Y-fronts, quiescent and taking the air only when I needed a pee.

Mrs Jha had never surfaced during these morning sessions. She was a late riser and there was an elderly aunt who loved getting Pralay ready for school. 'What to tell you, sir? I have to bathe him myself,' she said to me once. The twelve-year-old boy blushed brightly. I looked away quickly, pretending not to have noticed. If the old woman was getting her jollies by bathing this young man, if the young man was getting his jollies by being bathed by the old woman, who was I to interfere? But, of course, you can't confess without there being a fallout—the next time I went, the old lady was looking rocky and Pralay was looking sulky.

'What happened?' I asked Panna Mausi.

'Oh, he is all grown up now,' said Panna Mausi with a break in her voice. 'He does not need his mausi.'

'Oh, shut up,' Pralay said, but it was a plea—you could

tell. He drew out the 'up' so that it had three syllables and two tones.

'See how he talks!' said Panna Mausi. 'I am telling you, it is kalyug.'

I swear. She did say it. I never know whether it is Hindi films which write the dialogue for people's lives or people's speech patterns that determine Hindi film dialogue. I suppose there's a give-and-take.

'What did he do?' I asked.

'Nothing,' said Pralay sulkily

'Nothing,' said Panna Mausi tragically.

'I am twelve years old now,' said Pralay. 'I can take my own bath.'

'Sure you can,' I said. I felt bad for the old lady, but she had done herself in. I am sure that Pralay would have let her continue bathing him until his first pubic hair appeared if she had kept her mouth shut. But since she had needed to confess, he had had to cut her off.

That was perhaps the first time I realized that it was the House of Bernarda Alba. There was no masculine energy anywhere at all. Even the servants were women: tough, hard-working women from the villages, women who could carry a trunk on their backs and climb stools to pull heavy things off the tops of cupboards. Women with bodies so hard that you might mistake them for tree trunks, but women still. Pralay was the only man, but we know, don't we, that we all begin as women? The basic embryo is female until a burst of androgen turns it male. Again, once you're out of the womb, you spend your babyhood as a baby. Proud parents may say that they can see how sweetly feminine Gina-aged-six-months is or how macho and demanding Sohail-aged-seven-months is, but actually babies are babies. They are machines for eating and shitting and throwing up and sleeping. That's about it. Masculinity comes into play only with puberty.

And into this house of women without men I had walked.

Hmm.

Coffee at the Taj? I wanted to kick myself as I walked down the corridor to the lift, following the swing of that cute little tush in the tightly wrapped sari. I was looking at Prema's body now, and I realized that she was in great shape. She either took a great deal of care of it or she was naturally blessed. Her body had a curious golden hue, which she had imparted generously to her three children. And her hair was a nice thick rope down her back, not too much of it, not too little.

When we were ensconced in a bay window at the Taj's coffee shop, I took a careful look at her face. Wide forehead, nice eyebrows not picked too fine. Some laugh lines on either side of her eyes, a lovely brown, the colour of old amber. (Is there such a thing as new amber?) Her jaw was firm still and her neck was good. But her breasts—her breasts were truly magnificent. She let me have a look at them, dropping her pallu as she leant over the table to pick up a menu, and artlessly, so artlessly, she left it lying like a serpent across her stomach. The menu she held on her lap so that I could continue to look.

'How old are you?' I blurted out.

She looked at me for a moment. Then she dropped the menu and deliberately rearranged her pallu, bringing it studiously across her shoulders.

'Don't you know you should never ask a woman her age?' she said, continuing to maintain eye contact.

Was it the eye contact? Was it the sultry contralto? Was it the smell of jasmine wafting across the table? What was it about this innocuous remark that turned it into a catalyst? Why was I erect and aching? Why did I want to leap across the table and rip her blouse open and bury my face in between those lovely fragrant mounds of flesh? How much would they give? How much would they resist?

At one level, at an ordinary, rational level, I knew why I was reacting like this. I was a starving man in front of a feast.

I should explain.

When I joined college, I knew two things. I wanted to be a lawyer and I wanted to have money with which to get women into bed. I was, as most men at eighteen are, socialized enough to know that you couldn't do this just like that. You didn't get to have sex just because you liked a girl in your class and she liked you. You had to invite her out. She had to accept. You had to impress her. And this took money. I had some pocket money from my father, but he was the kind of man who didn't think anyone should have sex with anyone else until they were married, so he didn't factor that into my pocket money. He calculated my bus fare to college and added a hundred rupees a month as emergency money, just in case I needed to come home by taxi. If I spent any of my emergency money, I had to explain why or repay him. In three months' time, I was in debt and the fights were getting regular.

That's when I decided that I would give tuitions in mathematics. It is a subject I know. It is also a subject which has a steady demand. I didn't know at that point if I could teach it, but I did know that there was a market. Three years later, I was doing pretty well at it. I made enough money to bribe and seduce and impress a girl—I shall call her Sunayana and beg her pardon should she be reading this—so much that she actually allowed me to lick her cunt.

We were in her parents' bed at the time since they were away for the weekend. We had been kissing for hours, so my lips were dry and hers were beginning to hurt. Her breasts, she complained, were feeling like atta, with all the squeezing and rubbing that I had done. I bent down to kiss them, but she just pushed me wordlessly on. I worked my way down, past her stomach, her beautiful mound of a stomach, to the rough fur of her mons veneris. I tried to pull her skirt down, but she would not let me. I reached under it and found to my surprise and delight that she did let me. I pulled her panties off and began to explore her hair. At that moment, I came, firing repeatedly inside my pants, unable to control myself. My fingers dug into her and she yelped.

'Sorry,' I said. 'Sorry. Let me kiss it better.'

And before she could do a thing, I had burrowed under her skirt and pressed my face onto her. Of course, I knew I was near the destiny of my delight, but I didn't know its topography very well. Somewhere here, somewhere here. And then my angel guided me. Her fingers on either side of my head drew me to the sweet spot. Here was honey and lemon and fire. Here was my heart's desire. Here was a strange smell, so warm, so human, so woman. Here was hair and then, in the middle of it, a pink and brown nubbin, so intimate, so coy. I wanted to consume her. I wanted to snarl and snap and rip. Instead, I put out my tongue and touched her clit. It was a beautiful moment and I was ready again, my cock pushing against my pants, the orgasm I had just had forgotten except for a faint discomfort along the edges.

What would have happened that day? If Malti-the-maid had fallen and sprained her ankle and been unable to get to work? But Malti was surefooted and she arrived in the house and my angel was expelling me from paradise. However, I knew I was on my way.

And then my father threw a spanner into the works.

He died.

He died and, suddenly, I realized why he had fought me over every hundred-rupee note. We were a subsistence economy. We lived, the five of us, on his salary. He got it, we ate it. There was nothing in the bank. There was no money anywhere. And now my tuition money had to run the house.

I got to work. I increased the number of hours I was working. I increased the frequency of my visits. I raised my rates. And, within two months, I was handling the entire economy and managing to put away some money too.

But this meant the end of the relationship with Sunayana. She was a girl from a big house, as the saying goes, and she had the tastes that went with such a pedigree. Not for her coffee by the yard at an Udipi restaurant, oh no. It had to be an air-conditioned restaurant. Not for her a bunch of flowers created out of a walk through Malabar Hill, oh no. It had to be a glacial bouquet whose exotic qualities were emphasized by the cellophane wrapping and the curlicues of ribbon at its base. This should tell you that I tried these variants when I was trying to get back into the pairidaeza of her thighs. Didn't work. She went on a holiday to the USA, a long holiday, so long that when she returned she had a new wardrobe, a new nose and a ring on her finger.

After that, I threw myself into my work. Not because of a broken heart but because of my mother. She had always been a quiet figure in our house because she had not been allowed to talk much by my father. If she said anything at all, he would say, 'Go out and earn and then you can talk.' This was unfair because she was a tenth-standard pass and he had prevented her from studying further or working at anything. Incarcerated at home, she had forgotten what little English she had learnt. You might think this would have made her eager to make her daughters independent, but it didn't. She wanted them to be carbon copies of herself. She allowed them to get their degrees, but even while they were studying they were expected to come home immediately after classes were over. There were to be no extracurricular activities, no part-time work, nothing.

'Let them also work,' I said often. 'Let them contribute.'

Immediately, Mummy would turn on the tap. Your father would not have wanted them to work. Your father would not have allowed them to work. Your father would not have compromised their dignity.

After a couple of scenes like this, I decided that I would just have to earn their dowries and get rid of them. More work. More tuitions. From Pralay at seven-thirty in the morning right up to Moyna at nine-thirty in the evening, Sundays included, one hundred rupees an hour, all tax free. It added up, but not fast enough.

So I had had no time for romance. I was out of touch. I did not know how to talk to women unless they were mothers or elder sisters or mausis or chachis or phuphis or something like that.

'I'm sorry,' I mumbled at Prema. 'It's just that you look so young.'

She laughed, and suddenly I felt her knee touch mine under the table. You will think I am a duffer, but I moved mine away thinking it was a mistake. However, she was kind—or she was desperate. She moved hers back and this time she looked at me as she applied a deliberate and delicate pressure against my knee. My cock almost jumped out of my pants to salute her.

'Tell me about Pralay,' she said.

'Pralay?' I said. I almost added 'Pralay who?' but managed not to say it. Instead, I said the usual things I say: 'Pralay is a very bright boy. He can do very well if he chooses to. But he must choose to. I can only give him the tools.'

'I can imagine,' she said and bit her lower lip so quickly that I would never have been able to swear whether she had done it or I had imagined it.

But even if that fleeting expression had not crossed her face, even if it had only been me seeing what I wanted to see, by now I was sure. Mrs Jha was flirting with me. I did not know what to make of this, but I was intoxicated. I wanted her more than I had ever wanted Sunayana. I wanted her more than I wanted my sisters to get married and move out of the house. I wanted her more than I wanted to take my mother on a trip to that city in the north and discover that she wanted to stay behind, a corpse-throw away from the great river. But I also knew that she was my employer. She would set the rules of play. It was her game.

'So, you know what they say about taking a horse to water, but not being able to make it drink?' I said.

She nodded seriously. 'I have no problem with that. You are good for him. He needs a man in the house.'

I smiled.

'I do too,' she said.

I was beginning to feel my groove come back.

'Surely that shouldn't be a problem. A beautiful woman like you.'

She laughed. 'But, you see, I am beginning to think that I am not using my mind. I would like to take lessons in French.'

'Yes, that's a good idea. The Alliance Francaise…'

'I would like to take lessons from you.'

Then it dawned on me. From where I was standing, she was a rich woman, a free woman, who could live her life as she pleased. But she probably wasn't. She had to manufacture a reason for us to meet.

'Shall we start right away?'

'No, not today. This is the time when the house is empty. Mausi goes to the temple and Nita goes with her. The kids are in school or college, so we can do lessons without interruption.'

Nita was probably the maid, one of those women with the tree-trunk bodies and the rock faces, who looked like they had been born to be drudges. Eleven o'clock suited me as well. It was the time when everyone was in school, whether they had morning shift or afternoon shift or nine-to-four timings. It was generally the time that I spent sitting in the USIS library, trying to get serious about a law degree that I was doing part-time.

'Okay. Tomorrow?'

'Yes, tomorrow will be good.'

We finished our tea and for the first time in my life I ate

Taj ka khaana—but I cannot remember any of it. I don't know what they put in front of me; I ate it all without tasting a thing.

Outside, in the sea air, now warm against our faces, she said, 'What do you eat for breakfast?'

'Jo bhi,' I said.

'Non-veg?'

'Sometimes.'

'Please don't eat non-veg tomorrow morning,' she said. 'Can I drop you somewhere?'

She was again my employer. I tried to let my arm rest against hers in the car, but she withdrew it studiously. This was going to be a risky business. That added a certain zest to it—as if any more were needed.

The next morning, I debated masturbation seriously before I went in for my bath. I did not want to embarrass myself the way I had with Sunayana. My recovery time would have probably saved the day if Malti-the-maid had not destroyed it, but I didn't think I was going to be able to do the same this time. So, although my cock was hard—it had been hard through the night—I only washed it carefully and soaped my pubic hair three or four times.

It was warm when I stepped out and I hoped I wasn't going to sweat. Of course, if you hope that you aren't going to sweat you become aware of every drop, and each drop adds to your certainty that you are smelling terrible. I spend a huge amount of time in the sun. This means that I sweat. Because I am human. But I had learnt to carry a can of deodorant with me to mask the smell of my humanity. And so, in the middle of a pleasant daydream in which Prema Jha's silky black hair was caressing my hips as she brought her ruby-red lips down to my cock, I imagined her wrinkling her nose in disgust at the smell and withdrawing. I went to the bathroom and sprayed the deodorant into my pubic hair.

I almost screamed aloud. Only the thought of the child sitting a few feet away in his bedroom, waiting for me to come out and assign him homework, stopped me. My entire pubic region was on fire. The deodorant was stinging madly. I had grown accustomed to the burning sensation when I sprayed my armpits; I had not bargained for the fact that the skin below the belt had not been sprayed like that before.

My hard-on, which had not subsided for the last twenty-four hours, vanished magically. For once, I could tuck my three back into my underwear without having to wiggle and pray that nothing was going to go wrong.

At the Jha residence, at 11 a.m. sharp, Prema opened the door for me. I went inside and turned towards the dining room where I normally taught Pralay.

'Nah,' she said, cutting the word off at the end. 'This way.'

And I stepped into her bedroom.

It was an odd room. The floor was marble, but the bed was a cot. It was covered with a couple of plain rough sheets. There was a cupboard from which the mirror had been removed.

'A widow's world,' she said. She seemed to be watching me. 'Welcome.'

'You can't be serious,' I said.

'I am. This is how I live.'

Then she walked into my arms and I was kissing her violently, possessively.

'Arre,' she said 'Slow down. You cannot leave marks.'

'I don't see how that is possible,' I said. This was getting easier. 'Your skin is like a peach.'

'You fool.' She laughed. 'You can't leave marks where they will show.'

I bent down to kiss her neck.

'Never the neck,' she said. 'The neck is always difficult to explain.'

I lifted the weight of her black hair, which had not been twisted into a plait and hung down her back. I kissed her on the nape of her neck.

'Not here,' I said. 'Here I can do what I want.'

She moved a little in my embrace and I learnt over the next few weeks that this was how she showed her approval of what I was doing. She would not moan aloud; she had schooled herself not to. She was one of those strong, silent women.

This also meant that she set the pace. She knew how much time we had and she wanted to make the best use of it. So she brought my head back to her mouth and began to fiddle with the buttons of my shirt. I took it off quickly and then began to fumble with the hooks of her blouse. She slipped out of it and, suddenly, I was in possession of her breasts. They were beautiful, full, pliant, gorgeous. Most of all, what was beautiful about them was that they were real. They had not been photographed by someone else and printed by someone else. They had not been invented in the middle of my bath. They were here, they were real, they were mine. I could do with them what I wanted because they would be covered again by cloth and so would be safe. (Later, I would discover the uses of a needle in a situation such as a love bite.)

'Are you going to look at me all day?' she asked and began to twist her thighs together.

I moved quickly, almost falling out of my clothes.

'The condom?' she asked, and I could have screamed my frustration aloud.

I had forgotten about the condom. And it was obviously my responsibility. Mine alone. A woman in her position could scarcely be expected to go out and buy condoms. No woman could.

'Shit,' I said.

'Never mind,' she said. 'There are still some things we can do without one.'

I could have kicked myself. She was going to give me a handjob and send me on my way. But when we lay down on the cool floor, she began by kissing my shoulders and licking her way down into my chest hair. She nipped at my nipples, startling a yip from me.

'But make sure you don't do that to me,' she said with a mock-warning. 'I am very sensitive there.'

I took her seriously, not knowing that it was her way of asking me to do precisely that. I had a lot to learn about the ways of women.

She kissed me languorously and long and once or twice my body bucked so much that I thought I was going to come. My dick was leaking madly—pre-cum, thank the stars. And then she raised her body away from mine and lay back on the floor.

'My turn,' she said, and I rose to the occasion. I made sure I kept the lower half of my body away from hers because I did not trust myself to let my body touch hers—I might go off like a shot.

Finally, when I was licking her clit, there was a moment of surcease. She began to thresh about, she began to buck her hips, and when I made bold to suck deeply of her inner thigh, she came in an unmistakable manner.

It is impossible to explain how magnificent I felt at that moment. I was on top of the world. I had conquered Mount Everest. I had run a four-minute mile. I had won a Nobel Prize in fucking.

When she lay limp beside me, she reached for my organ.

'Never mind,' I said. 'Not today.'

And I watched with delight as a line of confusion marked

her brow. The delight expanded to include superiority. I had brought her to orgasm and I had left her dazed. I slipped out of the house after a quick wash.

The next day was a Pralay session. He handed me an envelope. Inside it were ten hundred-rupee notes.

I had been paid.

I had been paid for sex.

I had been paid well for sex.

I had never used a prostitute—sex worker, I should say—but I remember crossing the Oval Maidan late one night and being accosted by one. 'Hand mosan ka paanch rupaiya. Moonh mein dus rupaiya,' she had said. A handjob for five rupees had seemed like a good deal, except that I had caught a glimpse of her face and lost any desire to be serviced by her. She was well past her prime and had painted her face as if she were a clown: red daubs on her cheeks, blue eyeshadow and black streaks near her eyes.

I was now her brother under the skin.

I should have felt bad about this, but I didn't. I felt magnificent. It would go, I told myself with a chuckle, towards the dowries of my sisters. It was not for me, it was for them. I even laughed a little at my own hypocrisy.

Late that evening, I got a telephone call. It was Prema Jha.

'Can we have another French lesson next week?' she asked.

The house was quiet around me. All my family was asleep.

'Yes,' I said. 'This time we can start with a French letter.'

She didn't get the joke. She didn't have to. I did.

I wish I could say that I performed as well again, but I should have known that pride goeth before a fall. (Not that I have ever understood that. Surely pride goeth after the fall?) As soon as I arrived with my hard-won pack of condoms—this was in the time of Nirodh, when going into a chemist's shop to ask for a prophylactic was like shouting 'I'm having sex! I'm having sex!' and aunties would crane their heads around uncles to look at who the besharam behaya jaanwar was—we were at it. I almost tore Prema's blouse, but she didn't seem to mind. She was an inventive lover. One of the defining moments for me was when she raised my arm and began to lick my armpit.

I had no idea that the armpit could be so erogenous. I had no idea that there was a direct nervous connection between my groin and my armpit. I had no idea that a woman could lick so lovingly and just when I had got used to this, inasmuch as anyone can get used to the sensation of having one's cock tickled from within, she opened her mouth and took the fleshy bulb in and bit down, gently but firmly. I moaned so loudly that she had no option but to raise her body and suppress the sounds of my pleasure with one of her ample breasts.

I want here to think about her nipples. They were beautiful and pink. I have always felt a great enjoyment of the colour of nipples. They are so various and beautiful that when I am at a bus stop or a train station I spend my time assigning colours and shapes to the nipples of the women passing by. Hers must be pink and tiny, almost hidden in the yellow-whiteness of her breast. Hers are dark, almost black, and the areolae must be large and diffuse. I bless this breast with a pert mole at the corner of the breast and wonder at the magnificence of construction of these two. I look at the shapely and the shapeless and I think about their nipples.

Prema's were, as I have said, beautiful and pink. The nipples themselves had given in to the demands of time and the imperatives of three urgent mouths sucking at them. Three? Surely her husband must have feasted too? He made four. And then there was me, five. But this did not matter to me. I loved the random bumps and contours of her multinipples and the way the areolae grew flushed and hot under the demands of my mouth, as they bore bravely the impertinences of my tongue and the abrasion of my teeth. I loved the way there was no real demarcation between nipple and breast, just a fading away of the roseate hue, from ashes-of-roses to salmon-pink to flesh.

It was all too much for me, this investigation of my body, the way she had of making her body into a worshipping of mine. I entered her and my heart sang and the blood thundered in my ears. This was conquest. This was her surrender. This was my blooding. This was how I was to enter the ranks of men.

You never forget your first pay packet. You never forget your first fuck. I learnt that later. What I learnt at that moment was that it is better to think about all this at leisure. If you want to be a good lover—and which man doesn't?—it is best not to think about fucking when you are fucking. At that time, you should distract yourself and think about other things. Think about the seventeen-times table or try and list the chief ministers of your state in order. Try and take your mind off the fact that you are doing what every man would rather be doing. If you think about fucking when you're fucking, you'll find you're not fucking any more.

In other words, you'll come.

That's what happened to me. Almost as soon as I entered her, I was done. I groaned and buried my face in her hair.

'Ho gaya?' She seemed matter-of-fact.

I nodded and rolled off and hid my face under my arm. And then she taught me a lesson.

'Hey, I'm not done here,' she said. She grabbed the arm and pulled it off my forehead. 'Get on with it.'

I did, but it wasn't the same. When you're hot and wanting it, you don't notice anything, you just want it all. You want the softness of hair and the rhythm of muscle under skin. You feel like she is the most beautiful woman in the world, you feel like she is the most desirable of all possible lays. But when you've dropped your load and your cock is shrivelling in the condom and you're beginning to wonder if it's going to leak on the floor, you begin to notice that there are three hairs on one nipple and you wonder if it is because of age. As you run your fingers through her pubic hair, you look now for signs of ageing. You see the sag of the triceps and the folds of cellulite on the upper thigh. You should not be noticing. You should be rejoicing. Is this not the woman you dream about? Is this not the moment that you have been savouring as you walked from house to house, as you witnessed the titanic struggle of Tehmi with trigonometry? How can you be so choosy, so particular, when only a month ago you would have given a couple of teeth for this moment?

However, Prema Jha seemed to know what turned her on. She was good at leading me to the spot marked X and telling me how to do what I needed to in order to get her where she wanted to go. I added some variations of my own, sometimes startling her, sometimes displeasing her, but almost never disconcerting her in the way I had on the first day, that first time.

How long did we go on like this? I suppose I could tell by looking at my bank account. I had decided that the money I made from my cocksmanship would go towards myself and I opened a separate bank account so that I could put the money away there. As soon as I was done, I made a bank run and tucked it away, out of my reach. When the bank issued me a cheque book, I took it and ceremoniously hurled it into the Arabian Sea. I was not going to touch that money.

There was a time when French lessons sometimes happened twice a week, and the money kept coming. And then, quite by accident, I discovered a way to make a little more.

One day, my mother complained that she was not feeling well. When I asked, she went coy on me and said that she could not explain. By this, I took her to mean that it might be gynaecological and I asked the sisters to take charge. They did, but the news was not good. Mummy had a large tumour inside her. It was the size, the doctor said, of a coconut. It had to be removed immediately and, with it, her uterus too. I thought that this would not be too much of a problem for a woman her age. She had been through an early menopause and so her uterus was pretty much not a functioning part of her body. It would be like taking her appendix out.

But on the day that she was to go to the hospital, she was found sitting on the bed, in a flood of tears. The sisters thought she was in pain, but she was not. She was weeping and would not say why. I thought she was weeping for the loss of her womanhood. I tried to imagine myself as an eighty-year-old man whose cock and balls have not done anything for him for ten years. But still he might have some issues if someone threatened to cut them off.

I sat down next to Mummy and tried to explain hormone replacement therapy, but she was not listening to me. She was crying and making sounds like a child. I had a flashback to my father sitting with her on the bed and trying to explain something to her and failing. He had taken her in his arms and cuddled her and hummed to her as if she were a child, so that was what I did. Finally, she stopped sobbing and the sisters stopped bobbing in and out like helpless ducks and I discovered what the matter was.

Nothing was the matter. She knew that the operation was routine. She knew that the tumour was probably benign. But she was scared. She told me about so-and-so who had gone in for a tooth extraction and had bled to death. She told me about such-and-such who had had a bad case of appendicitis and had come through the operation okay and was about to go home when he had developed a slight fever and then spent three days in the ICU and then died of organ failure. She told me about someone who had never drunk or smoked but had had a stroke while taking a blood test.

'Hospitals are there to kill you,' she said.

And it came down to this. She would go to the hospital, but only if all three of her children were there and if all three of them were visible to her when she went into the operation theatre because this might be the last thing she would ever see in her life.

I agreed.

So I made a hurried call to Prema Jha. Only, she did not pick up the phone, and I could not tell the old mausi who did what I wanted to say—that there would be no class that day. So I just did not go and instead went with my mother to the hospital.

I thought at first that I might be able to get away in time, but the admission process took hours. There was always another form to fill and another person to meet and another place to go and someone else to register with. But finally it was done and Mummy was wheeled into the operating theatre. My sisters began to cry noisily until I snapped at them and announced that I had to go and earn a living and they had better pull themselves together.

'When will you come back?' the older one asked.

'I don't know,' I said. 'Usual time.'

But, instead of going for tuitions, I just went home. It was lovely to be at home, alone. I made myself two sandwiches—one of bread and ghee and sugar and the other of bread and butter and the rasa of mango pickle—and a big cup of tea. Then I sat down in front of the television set and put in a video cassette of *Sholay*. I felt good and relaxed.

Then the phone rang. I picked it up and heard: 'Teri baahon mein hai jaanam, meri jism-o-jaan pighalte.' I hung up and started the film again. The phone rang after about five minutes and there it was again. Another Hindi film song playing: 'Tum bin jaaoon kahaan?' I began to wonder what was happening. The third time, I listened to a verse of the song and then said, 'Hullo?'

It was Prema.

'Why didn't you come today?'

I didn't know what to say. I thought I could tell her the truth, that my mother was in the hospital. But I was silent. Perhaps because the next question would be: 'So what are you doing at home?'

'I had some work,' I said.

'Oh,' she said. 'I'm sorry to hear that.'

Her voice was cold. I grew angry.

'Yes, I have to earn a living,' I said. 'I have a mother in the hospital and two sisters to marry off. I have a home loan to pay. Are you sorry to hear that as well?'

I banged the phone down.

I felt good. I felt bad. I had told the truth. I had lied. I had showed the rich bitch her place in the world. I had pushed away the only woman I knew who would give me sex for free. I could barely concentrate on the movie.

And then the sisters came home and began shouting about who had left the butter out of the fridge, and why had I left the spoon in the pickle, didn't I know it would get black?

That was when I knew that I had to get out of there. I had to find another home. I had to find another way to live.

The next morning, I was supposed to teach Pralay. To my surprise, Prema was also awake. Her eyes were swollen. If I had known then what I know about women now, I would have known that she had managed this somehow. But I was young and I was guilty. So I felt sorry for her.

'Sir, my math tests ka results,' said Pralay. I looked at them cursorily. Normally, this would be a time of some tension. Good marks mean you get to continue. Bad marks may even mean dismissal, although most parents will listen to some nonsense about their son having what it takes and just not paying attention, etc., etc. Pralay seemed to have done well. Sixty per cent was okay. In normal circumstances, I would have sighed and read him a little lecture over the missing forty per cent. Instead, I gave him a dazzling smile and said that he had done very well and watched with alarm as he responded with visible enthusiasm.

This was a turning point for Pralay, and I discovered it only by accident. You don't have to wait for ninety per cent to compliment the kid. You can do it when they've shown some improvement, and this gets them hooked. They want your approval—and they will work for it.

Idiots.

But it is idiocy that makes us all manageable. Prema's idiocy made her manageable too, for now she produced a watery smile and a Rolex watch.

'This is for you, sir,' she said. 'From all of us.'

'And I get nothing?' Pralay said.

For a moment, I looked at the watch and I thought to myself: 'Now you are a gigolo. This is exactly the kind of gift a rich woman gives to a gigolo.' And then I looked at the watch again and thought: 'That's only a word. I don't have to call myself anything I don't want to call myself.'

But my middle-class mind was still active and so, before I could stop myself, I was saying, 'I don't need anything for doing my duty.'

For a moment, venom flashed in Prema's eyes and she looked like she was going to take me seriously. Then Pralay saved the day.

'I need a watch, Mama,' he began to whine. 'And it's not fair. I did the work. I got the marks. And sir gets the watch. I don't see why I…'

So I got to take the watch. The whole family insisted, except for Mausi, who was looking on with clear eyes.

When I was leaving, she said, 'Sir, where you are going?'

I said I was going to the USIS to study. It was the truth.

'Sir, I am going that side only. I will give you drop.'

This seemed a little puzzling because Mausi did not appear to care much for me. I had thought this was a caste thing—that I, a Kayastha, was eating at her Brahminical table—but now she didn't seem to mind dropping me in her car?

'That flat?' she said, pointing across the corridor as we left the flat. 'Police are coming there.'

'Oh?'

'You know why?'

'No.'

'Because one gold bangle is going missing. There was one servant they had. He is a nice boy. A young boy. Big-made. Whatever work, he will put his hand. Not saying, no, for this I am not here, for that I am not here. He is just doing and helping.'

'Good. Such people are rare.'

'Haan, but that is first-first. Later, he is changing. He is becoming…how you say?' She frowned and pulled down the sides of her mouth.

The lift arrived.

'Surly?'

'Haan. Perfect.' She pronounced it to rhyme with 'defect'. 'He is becoming surly. This word I must learn because it is happening a lot to our servants.'

We got into the lift and went down five floors.

'You see, it is the way of the world,' she said. 'Servants are servants. This is how it is. How can we change the world?'

Bitch. But I felt that there was no way to argue with her. So I simply said, 'One cannot.'

'It is good for all of us to remember that,' she said. She stopped at the entrance to the building, where the names of the owners were inscribed on wooden plates in a variety of paints and fonts that could probably tell you something about the owners. 'P. Jha', it said in plain Roman. 'This house is in my name.'

'Really?'

'Haan. P here is for Panna, not Premlata.'

'Premlata?'

'She,' she said and jerked a thumb over her shoulder. 'Premlata, she was. After Baba, she began calling herself Prema.'

'After Pralay?'

'No, after Praveen.'

Praveen, I assumed, was the dead husband.

'Here,' she said, pointing to the ground beneath her feet. 'They found him here.'

'Who?'

'You don't know? Praveen. They found him here. When he fell.'

'Fell?'

'Five years ago. He fell. It was the first time the police came to the building. For us. For the Jhas.'

I tried to arrange my face to look sympathetic, but I was actually quite shocked. These things didn't happen in such buildings, did they?

'I told first only. I told Badi Bi,' continued Mausi.

'Who is Badi Bi?'

'She lives in that house. She owns it. I said, "If the boy is from the hills, he will be fair and he will be tall. Your son is here, there, here, there. But your bahu is here all the time." But she said, "I am here to see." Haan, we are there to see, but we are not there twenty-four hours. Some time for God. Some time to sleep. Some time to go and see sick friend. That is when it happens. I told her.'

I had thought she had been talking about the neighbours. Now I wondered.

'Then Badi Bi saw. It was getting bad. He would not give tea. He would put down tea like this, like you're giving a gali ka kutta some roti. He asked for one television set. When they did not give, he would put on television himself. And sit. In front. Arre, some servants in this building forty years, like that. They won't sit. He was sitting. Haq se. And the bahu was there.'

I sighed. I had no idea where this was going.

'Then it happened.'

'What?' I asked.

'Badi Bi lost her bangle. A big gold bangle. She called the police. They came and they searched the boy's boriya-bistar and they found the bangle in the middle of it. Just like that. How much he was crying, I did not do, I did not do. How much he was weeping when they took him away. I am told they beat him and beat him until he confessed.'

I felt a chill of horror down my spine.

'You see, you can say this is gone, you can say that is finished. You can say things are not like they used to be. But one thing is left. Police knows whose word to take. Badi Bi's word? Or the word of some boy from the village?'

She was warning me. The silly bitch was warning me. I lashed back.

'Whose word did they take? When they came for Praveen?'

I saw hatred in her eyes, clear as the full moon on Shivratri. She was declaring war on me.

'They took her word. They took my word. We said: "He went to hang up some lights and he slipped." That is what we said. But I know and she knows.'

What was she saying? That Praveen had been pushed? That he jumped? It was all getting too complicated for me. I got out of the car and then leant down to look in at the window of the ancient Ambassador.

'Thank you for your advice. Should I return this watch or will you go to the police?'

She smiled.

'That is your inaam. Pralay did better in mathematics. You may keep it.'

'And I'll even tell him to let you give him bath,' I said and I saw her face whiten and go taut. It was unfair and unkind, but the bitch was cutting me off.

I walked down to the arcade and asked about the prices of Rolex watches. It was incredible how different the price ranges were when you wanted to buy and when you wanted to sell. I asked after the older watches and found that I might get a better price were I to keep it for a while. I gave up the idea of selling it immediately and converting it into cash. There's something about cash that I like. It is what you want it to be. A watch, on the other hand, on whichever hand, is a watch. But I suppose it was better than burfi.

Because that was all I had been getting when the kids did better.

Burfi.

Often it was good burfi, but burfi nonetheless. So I began to show my Rolex to other parents when I thought that their tykes were doing well. I managed to score a nice pen, a silver card case and a rather lovely tie-pin simply by playing on the idea that it was the done thing to give the teacher something nice and non-edible, something to remember the child by when it was all over. These, I quickly turned into cash, and the cash into bits of gold. No stones, no beads, no shares. I like gold and I would buy it as soon as I could afford it and stick it in a safety deposit locker I had got for myself. The key? It was wrapped into a pair of socks.

The next time I went to meet Prema, I went up only when I saw the Ambassador trundle away with its burden of old women. Prema seemed to be eager for sex; she barely let me speak before she had me on the floor. I took her cue and gave it to her as she wanted it. My teeth were buried in the curve of her shoulder, my hips pumping frantically as she lashed her head from right to left. It was all over in a few minutes. When I reached between her thighs, she pushed my hands away. Obviously, she had managed to come.

'What did she say?' she asked.

I told her.

She stared at me.

'How did she know?'

'I told her,' I said sarcastically. 'How do I know? She has eyes in the back of her head. She has a spy in the building.'

'Hari Om!' she said.

'Hari Om!' I echoed.

'No, no, not like that. I mean, the building watchman. He is her pet dog.'

I sighed. 'Maybe it would be best to end this.'

'No, no, she cannot win. Let me think.'

I shrugged and got up and put on my clothes.

'Have a bath before you go.'

'No,' I said. 'I'm in a hurry.'

I don't know why I said it, nor do I know why I walked down the stairs when I left the building. Outside, I saw the Ambassador. I leant in and smiled at the driver.

'Kya hua?'

'Badi Mem ko chakkar aa gaya. Waapis aayi.'

She had thought to catch us red-handed. Someone up there was obviously looking after my interests. It was time to cut and run.

I gave Prema and Pralay one month's notice. Pralay didn't even notice. I had barely taught him a few months and there was no emotional bond between us. Prema was too sensible to want to jeopardize her position. She thought of various ways in which we could make it work. We could meet out of Bombay. Yes, we could, but that would mean going out of Bombay and I could not do that too often.

'I can give you what you will lose on the tuitions,' she said.

It wasn't quite that simple. A tutor who is irregular is no tutor at all. He loses reputation, he loses students and, eventually, he loses everything. I know. I've inherited a lot of these students. 'Sir, bas one thing,' one of the parents will say to me. 'Aap regularly aaya karo. That is all Munna needs. Regular.' I agree. It is almost always the answer. If you want to get better at something, do it regularly.

I suggested an easier way. She could hire me a small flat of my own. I could live there and she could visit whenever she wanted. She thought about that and then turned it down. She didn't have that kind of money. I looked at her.

She was living in a three-or-four-bedroom apartment that faced the sea. She could give me a Rolex watch when her son improved his maths score or I didn't turn up to service her. And she couldn't set me up in a love nest?

'It's not easy,' she said. 'I have to account for everything. The trust asks questions.'

Apparently, Praveen's death had raised many questions in the biradari. They had decided that his money would go into a trust. She got an allowance.

'If I handle it well, I can live well,' she said. 'But I can't afford anything like this.'

And so that was that.

I steadied myself with a long walk by the sea. I was not in love with Prema. I had enjoyed having sex with her. I had gained some money and a good watch. But I did not want to lose sight of my own objective. I wanted to earn enough money to buy my own house, to go back to my dream of becoming a lawyer. I would move on.

Nothing happened for a year or more. At least, nothing happened that would be of interest to relate here. I bought myself a second-hand motorbike, after much thought. I had resisted for a long time because I did not want to spend any money. Then I realized, after some calculations including the price of fuel, that it would mean savings for me. I could pack the students in closer instead of leaving fifteen-minute gaps for travel. I could sleep at least half an hour longer every day or spend more time in the gym, so there were even health benefits. My mother said it would be risky, but I knew that I was sensible and I would not go about riding like a madman. I want to live. The only downside was that my face got very dirty and so did my clothes—the dust blows and the wind forces it into the clothes—but the sisters were there to look after this. Besides, now I had some measure of freedom. I could travel anywhere in the city without thinking about how much time it would take.

The motorbike was also how I met Aparna.

She was standing at the bus stop at Nepean Sea Road, and she did not look like any of the other women who were standing there. For one thing, they were all in jeans and T-shirts and she was in a salwar kameez. It was not a khadi-type thing, but it was cotton. She didn't look like a rich South Bombay bitch. She stood out because she was a bit dark, but she didn't care—you could tell by how she held her body and how she stood. She knew she was beautiful.

I noticed that she got into a bus that was headed to Nana Chowk and I guessed that she was a Wilson College student. I didn't even think all this consciously, you understand, it was just going on inside my head. Haan, there she is, that indigo-blue-kurta girl again, only today it's black-and-red. And that bus, where will she be going? Okay, so...

One day, quite by chance, our eyes met. The next day, I sought out her eyes, but then I caught her glance and looked away. The next day, I smiled. Fourth-fifth day, she wasn't there. The day after, she was. I raised a hand and, before she could stop herself, she raised a hand too. And a couple of weeks after I had first noticed her, I stopped and said, 'Lift?'

One thing that always holds good in India: you cannot do anything on the quiet. The whole world stops to look at you. You would have thought that Amitabh Bachchan had come to pick up Hema Malini, the way everyone turned and looked.

'No, thank you,' she said.

'Come on,' I said. 'What can happen to you on a bike?'

She smiled and shook her head and didn't look at me. Great, I thought, and looked at the books she was holding against her chest. This is how all Indian girls stand: with their books in front of their breasts, so that roadside Romeos and cheapsters like me cannot get a good look or get a good feel.

The next day, I smiled, and she smiled back. But it was a yes-I-acknowledge-you-exist-but-don't-imagine-I-am-going-to-take-it-any-further smile. I didn't like that smile. So I just dipped my chin on the next couple of occasions that I passed.

To tell you the truth, I was rather busy elsewhere. After a few weeks, my luck seemed to be about to turn. I was teaching the sons of the owner of someone who made megabucks in a jink-mandi. I am joking, of course. This man was a metal dealer and he had made his money in zinc. He was now all set to take it global and he wanted his wife to be the kind of hostess who could speak English

Or so she said.

Her husband seemed to have very few opinions. He was a large man, not really obese, but one day his lungi fell open and his hairy thighs were visible. They were enormous, spreading at least a foot-and-a-half across. I felt a little sick looking at all that flesh and I promised myself that I would never let myself get that way. But already I could feel my muscle tone being compromised by the bike. I was riding it everywhere, as my friends had warned me I would. I fired it up to go to the market, which was about a hundred metres away from the house, for instance.

Mrs Jinks—as I will call her—was, in sharp contrast to her husband, a luscious lady. Everything about her was choice. She was in her early thirties and, though she wore only saris and kept her head covered, there was something about the way she moved that suggested something much more exciting. She was, I thought sometimes, like a river that is about to flood. Finally, she had hazel eyes. I find these unbelievably exciting. I don't know why. I know people say that people with light eyes are untrustworthy, but I don't believe it. Anyway, I didn't care. I was not looking for a life partner in her.

'When shall we study?' I asked and was immediately depressed when she asked if we could conduct the class directly after I had finished with Aniruddh. That meant she had no designs on my person. She was asking for a class in the middle of the evening, when the entire family would be present.

'Sorry,' I said. 'I won't be able to. That time is full up. How about eleven in the morning?'

'Tell him,' she said, and a certain feline satisfaction crossed her lips.

Mr Jinks looked bored. 'This means you will be coming two-two times?'

I agreed that I would.

'Arre, car bhej diya karo sir ke liye.'

I thought this uncommonly kind of him, but I saw the feline satisfaction evaporate. I began to suspect that these were rather deep waters. I had the feeling that I might get caught in a Roman Polanski script, where husband and wife do battle and some helpless third person gets caught in the middle.

But the helpless third person, I have thought, is always a bit silly. S/he can always walk away, and never does. I resolved that I would just walk away if things got too complicated.

I turned down the car politely.

'Arre,' said Mr Jinks, 'why?

I thought quickly. 'Sir, if the car is late, I am late. But if I am coming on my own, then I can always be on time.'

He looked unconvinced.

'Besides, your driver would have to come to a different place each time.'

'Haan, you go to different-different places,' he said, making me sound like someone slightly cheap.

But that wasn't him, I realized. It was me.

'Haan,' I said. 'Aaj kal, Saraswati gali-gali phirti hai.'

He looked abashed.

On the way out, I stopped to chat with the doorman. 'Jinks Saahab ka driver kaun hai?'

He looked at me, a slight expression of mistrust crossing his face. I offered him a pack of cigarettes. He took one and tucked it behind his ear. I had not seen anyone do that outside of the movies.

'Woh,' he said. 'Hero.'

I did a double-take. 'Woh?'

The man chuckled.

'Wohi,' he said. 'Ulti Ganga behti hai, bhaiya!'

He had pointed out a young man who looked like he was a film star. He had the jaw for it, certainly, and the carefully sculpted body. Nothing I could have done in the gym could have produced that effect. It was steroids and supplements, plus the genetic talent to keep it going. He was in spotless white, but his trousers were not the same material as his shirt, as befits those who wear uniforms for a living. He was wearing beige corduroy pants that seemed to have been stitched onto him, ridge by ridge.

'Naam kya hai?'

'Uska?' I thought of a snappy retort in the fashion of *MAD* magazine but decided against it. 'Armaan,' said the old man. He gave the word a slightly lewd tone. Was this the man I was replacing? Would he suddenly find a bangle in his glove compartment?

I felt a shudder run down my spine and then I thought of the swollen river, of my chances of taking a dip, and I stiffened my resolve. (I had stopped carrying a bag around after Panna Mausi's warning; it was irrational, I knew, because if someone is out to get you they're going to get you, but I was taking no chances.)

And so Aparna faded a little from my consciousness.

When you think there's the promise of sex, other things fade. Like love. Not that I was in love with Aparna—at that time, I did not even know her name, and I wasn't even sure that I wanted to know it. But I could tell from her clothes, from her bearing, from the way she held those books, that she was not going to fall into my lap and start undoing my zip. She would want a courtship and promises and dinner dates and all the rest of that. I was not averse to this. I can see why a woman might want such things and why a man might want to provide them for her, but I did not feel any pressing need to go down that road. 'Nalli saaf to sab kuchh maaf,' as my school buddies would have said.

Then one day, as I was riding down the road, I saw her wave at me. I waved back before I realized that hers was not a 'Hi' wave. It was a frantic wave. It was a wave that said: 'Stop, right now!' I could have ignored her and, truth be told, I was tempted to do so. After all, she had turned me down. And I could kind of guess that she wanted to go to college, while I was riding in the opposite direction. But I did slow down almost before I had made up my mind and then it was too late because she was beginning to run towards me and again her body language spoke of panic. To start again now, to ride off down Nepean Sea Road, would have been tantamount to slamming the door in her face. So I stopped, and she came running up to me.

'I have an examination in fifteen minutes,' she said. 'And I missed my bus.'

'Get on,' I said.

She got on and immediately I could smell her fragrance. It was nothing that came out of a bottle. Instead, it was all earth and mud and richness. It was shikakai and herbs. It was spicy and rich and completely feminine because there was a trace of sweat in it, the sweat of her panic. She was also, I was glad to see, no slippery side-saddle squatter. Instead, she threw her leg over the machine, and the next thing I felt were her arms looping around my waist and the pert thrust of her breasts against my back. I started the machine and we were off, south down Nepean Sea Road.

'Wrong way,' she shouted in my ear.

'Wrong way for the bus. Right way for you,' I shouted back. 'I'll get you to college in time.'

'This is not the way,' she shouted again as I wove between two cars and shot up the flyover near Priyadarshini Park.

'It is the way,' I shouted. 'Trust me'

We roared up Malabar Hill, and I ducked in and out of a school of Japanese tourists looking at an old Jain temple and then broke the signal at Walkeshwar and hurtled down the road past Birla School. Several schoolgirls raised a cheer. Aparna unlooped an arm to throw them a wave and a white smile that flashed in my rear-view mirror. Then she shook her head into the wind and turned her face up to the sun.

I broke another two signals at Chowpatty, and we roared to a halt in front of Wilson College.

'Thanks,' she said.

'You owe me,' I said, allowing a flash of naughtiness in my smile.

'I always pay my debts,' she said. Then she turned and ran.

And I rode off again, happy in an odd way, in a way that even a swollen river could not manage.

The river was running thick and fast when I got to the home of the Jinkses. The house was empty, which seemed a little odd, but Mrs Jinks was also subdued, which seemed as well. I suggested we use the children's bedroom where I taught the young Jinkses, but she pointed wordlessly to the dining table in the hall. This was a bit depressing. Was I going to have to teach English? Oh, well. If so, so.

I suggested we start with 'I am, you are, he is, she is…' I had learnt what little French I knew through conjugations and thought it seemed a good enough way to begin since few people who don't speak English fluently ever get their tenses right.

She limped along with me willingly. 'I em, you aarr, he ij, she ij,' she said and kept casting sideways glances at me, as if she were expecting me to make some move. Since we were sitting side by side, I moved my elbow so it touched hers. Almost immediately, she withdrew her arm. And still those glances, increasingly coy. If ever there were mixed signals, hamin ast, hamin ast, hamin ast. And yet, the idea of the paradise she was promising drove me on. Having had my arm repulsed, I decided to use my knee and slowly slid it against hers. Once again, her knee moved away. But the glances were now almost frantic, her colour high and her breathing fast.

I gave up. I thought she might be afraid, so I brought it all down a notch. I began to take on, almost without knowing it, the demeanour I had with her children. I was stern and severe and clicked my tongue irritably when she made mistakes.

And then her elbow slipped and began to rub against mine.

I grew brusque and began to make sounds as if she were a retard whose dimwittedness I could not believe.

And her knee came up to mine.

Then the hour was up, so I decided to punish her and snarled: 'You are completely stupid and I cannot teach you.'

'Sorry, sir,' she said. 'Very, very sorry.'

But she was crooning it and seemed ready to come.

'And if I am to come again, you cannot dress like this,' I said, pointing to her salwar kameez.

'How to dress then?' she asked in Hindi.

'This also I will have to teach you,' I said.

'Haan,' she said. 'Maybe you should teach me how to dress too.'

I suspected irony and found none.

'Next time,' I said.

And when she turned around, I gave her a smart slap on her rear. She gasped and stood still, so I tried again. But there were too many layers between my hand and her for this to be any fun for me, even if it was clear that she was enjoying it. I decided to leave it alone for the moment.

'Ja rahe ho?' she asked as I prepared to leave.

I grabbed her by the shoulders and pushed my face into hers. 'Why should I stay? Yahaan rakha kya hai?' I smashed my lips against hers and, for a moment, she simply waited me out. And then the river burst its banks. Her tongue surged into my mouth, her fingers dug into my back and she raised one leg and coiled it around the back of my thigh, pushing her crotch into mine. We were evenly matched in height, we were evenly matched in passion, but something told me that it would not be a good idea to take this straight to the bedroom now.

'Chudail,' I said as I detached my mouth from hers. 'Rundi,' I whispered as I ran my tongue from cheek to ear. 'Daayan,' I said as I nipped the earlobe from which a solitaire dangled. I was so close to her that I could see the blood running under her skin. 'And this is for punishing me,' I said, pulling away.

I left, although she was moaning for more.

The next time, she was as good as her word. She was wearing only a huge Turkish towelling robe, which I could see had come out of a Taj Mahal Hotel. It is incredible how cheap the rich can be. However much there is to be made in metal, they will try and get a little more for their money's worth, a towel here, a bathrobe there. I promised myself I would never do that kind of thing when I was rich.

She beckoned me into her bedroom.

'What I will wear?' she asked. She said wear to rhyme with here.

I thought I might correct her, but she had dropped her towel and was facing me, naked. She was reflected in the mirrors of her wardrobe, so I could see her reflected, every view I could want.

There is an Indian woman who is seen as cosmopolitan. Indeed, she is. Her hair ripples like silk and her walk promises the magic of a woman who is willing to look you in the eye while sucking on your big toe. But the rest of her body has withered into a reptile. She has lost weight and turned into a stick insect. This means she pleases no one but herself—and how often we are told that she dresses, she uses make up, she does whatever she does to her body, only for herself.

But here, in front of me, was the wish-fulfilment of any Indian man. Here was a woman willing to transform herself into the houri of his desires. Here was a woman in the fullness of her womanly splendour: her hair was that black silky river and her eyes were electric with desire, her lips were parted—but who cared about all that? I could not look above her breasts and beneath her hips. Here was delight.

'You do not have to dress,' I said. 'Today we will study parts of the body.'

She pretended to look coy and reluctant. This, you can imagine, must have been something of a feat since she was nude and had dropped her dressing gown voluntarily. But then, almost at the moment that I was going to give in, I realized that this was part of her game.

'You are not going to obey me?' I snarled, and she began to cower against the wardrobe. I pulled her into my arms and, for an instant, I was almost overwhelmed by the feminine pulchritude in my arms. But I caught hold of myself.

I was not here to enjoy myself, I told myself only half-mockingly. I was here to earn myself a house so I could enjoy it later. And how would I enjoy myself then? I had to shake away the thought of my father and my mother and the three of us, all living together, all of us locked into a nightmare of modern city life, where you send your children to the movies when you want to cop a feel of the wife to whom you are legally married.

I forced the thought out of my mind. If I were to pay attention to it, what might happen? All my life, I had seen myself as a certain person, and that certain person had a certain way of getting ahead. This involved getting married and having kids and having a house and having a career. As I bit into Rewa's neck, why did this seem like a plan that had belonged to someone else?

She was moaning by the time I reached down to pinch

a berry-pink nipple with my fingers. I pushed her down so that she was crouching in front of me. And then I turned her head and ground it into my crotch. She looked up at me and said, 'Nahin, woh main nahin kar sakti.'

I kicked her from me and pretended to walk away. She lay on the ground moaning but caught hold of my ankle.

'Acchha, baba,' she said. 'Jo tumko ho pasand, wohi karenge.'

I sat down on the edge of the bed and looked at myself in the mirror. Here I was, sitting on the bed of a room where each square foot cost more than my monthly wages. Here was the co-owner of this house, squatting nude between my feet. She reached for my belt, but I pushed her away.

'Start with my feet,' I said, and she looked confused. I translated, and she got it. She was a quick study and was licking my toes eagerly in a moment, spread out in front of me like a slave. I had never, in all my solitary morning excavations into the world of my fantasies, ever thought up something like this. My fantasies were drawn from Hindi films: Hema Malini tearing my shirt and jeans open as she slid, her feet torn by glass, down the front of my body; Sridevi rippling her body against mine and discovering the thorns that would stab her...that kind of thing.

And I knew what I had to do.

'Stop it,' I said. 'Enough.'

And I got up and left.

Like that.

I don't know why, but it was the perfect thing to do.

When I went to teach the little Jinkses, another watch happened. I had begun to understand how to function.

I wore the watch to have coffee with Aparna. I took her to the Sea Lounge; it seemed like the thing to do. She had protested in the way women do. 'Oh, it's too expensive,' she had said when I called her at her friend's house. (I wasn't allowed to call her at home, she hadn't even given me her number, what if her family found out about me?) At the same time, she had also managed to convey her excitement about being taken to a posh joint, her realization that she had to matter to me for me to take her there.

Did she matter then? I don't think so. I took her there because I could. It felt good to be able to waste money.

'You have a great watch,' Aparna said, sitting at a window-side table, looking out to the sea. 'It's an antique, I think.'

'How do you know?'

'My father has a collection of watches,' she said. 'I've seen one like that. It costs a lot.'

I looked at the watch again and with more respect.

The next time I went to the Jinkses, I wore the watch. Rewa was again nude, but I said carelessly, dismissively, 'Put on some clothes.'

'Why?'

'Because I say so, bitch,' I said and slapped her on the buttocks.

She flushed and went off to change. I followed her.

'No,' she protested. 'You don't look.'

I leant down casually and bit her nipple. Hard.

'No?' I asked.

'No,' she said again, this time flinging a challenge at me.

I grabbed her and dragged her to the bed. I sat down on it and pulled her across my knees. And then I spanked her. She gasped and began to wriggle. Her thighs began to twist against each other, like copulating snakes. A few more strokes, and she had had an orgasm. How do I know? It was unmistakable, the way her body bucked and rocked, as if every bone inside it were possessed of a desire to move in the direction opposite to the bone next to it.

She rolled off my knee.

'Padhaai karein?' I asked.

She looked startled and then she smiled. She went to the wardrobe, but I said, 'Nahin, come like that only.' She looked even more startled, but walked nude, elegant, in control, to the dining room and to the table.

'There is only one way to learn a language,' I said. 'You must talk it.'

She cocked her head and smiled at me. She was so stunning and that smile was so effective, I wondered why she would need to learn any language at all. She would be able to win friends, influence people and do whatever she wanted, if she could only keep smiling like that. Perhaps it helped that she was in the nude and that her breasts were sitting on the edge of the table, like two plump doves.

'Okay,' she said.

'So talk.'

'Do you like vaatch?'

'Did you like the watch?' I corrected.

'Did you like the vaatch?' she parroted.

'Yes, I liked the watch,' I said and stroked one of the doves.

'It is my father,' she said.

'It belonged to my father,' I said.

'Belong?'

I explained.

'You belong me,' she said.

How does anyone ever learn a language they haven't learnt as a child?

'No,' I said. 'You belong to me,'

'Wohi toh.'

'Stand up,' I said.

She did. The seat of the chair was wet. Her essence.

I ran a finger in it.

'Chhee,' she said.

'Clean it up,' I said.

She moved to get a cloth.

'No,' I said, a master again. 'With your tongue.'

As she crouched there, I undid my trousers and pulled out my cock. I got a condom on without tearing it—some feat, that—and bent over her. I thrust into her and she screamed, but more for effect than out of pain, I thought. I began to fuck her as a dog might fuck a bitch, hard and fast. She was so wet that I could barely keep my cock from slipping out of her. When I felt my orgasm roaring into my head, filling my body with its heat, I let my body drop onto hers. She bore me heroically.

Then the lesson was done and I left with a pair of cufflinks. I did not know if they belonged to her father. I didn't care. They seemed to be made of gold. Of course, they weren't. They were gold-plated and the stone in them was badly flawed. Net worth? Much less than the watch.

It was time to be cruel so that I could be kind to my bank account.

And so, for a week, I cut her off. I did not visit the house. I did not see the children.

Finally, on Sunday, a call came. One of my sisters took it and said, 'It's from the father of one of your pupils.'

This was rare. Education was part of what some jocular men would call the home minister's portfolio. In other words, when the children did well, they would claim the credit. When the children did badly, it was the mother's negligence. As for all the paraphernalia involved in education, in the selection and paying of tutors, all that was also part of what wives did.

Thank heavens for that.

It made my job a little easier.

'Sir, aap to aate nahin hai?' said Mr Jinks.

I explained that I had not been well.

'Sir, you tell to me the real problem. Armaan has seen you in the area, day-night, day-night. Means you are well to teach other's children. Why not mine?'

Armaan again.

'Well,' I said. 'I will talk to you businessman to businessman. I have been offered more money...'

'Arre, since when we are kanjoos? Take the money you want, tell what it is, we will give. Now, please, you start tomorrow.'

I did indeed start again the next day with the little Jinkses. I gave one of them the cufflinks and told him to give them to his mother.

'Kiska hai?' he asked, slightly suspicious.

'Speak English or you get a kattoos,' I said. I find that boys respond well to the threat of violence. It makes them feel like men. I would not administer the knuckles-to-forehead, but just the threat of it keeps them in line. Girls are easier; sarcasm is cheap and effective.

'Like kattoos is English, na?' he replied. I rather liked him, the little Jinks. He had his mother's skin and eyes. More than that, he had charm—and this came out of not being loved enough. This made him want to please you and wanting to please you meant he tried a little harder.

'Who is this?'

'Whose are these?' I corrected him.

'Wohi toh.'

I gave up the unequal struggle.

'You'll get punished. They are your mother's. She lent them to me.'

He opened the box.

'It is nice.'

'I know.' I said. But I did not add: 'They are valueless.

And I prefer old watches with value to cufflinks that look nice but are gold-plated with flawed stones and have no brand name attached.' He might have thought the less of me.

'They were my father,' she said the next day, her eyes a bit red. I wondered if she had been weeping for me or if she had organized a little redness of eye in order to persuade me that she had been weeping. We had finally got around to body parts and I had derived much pleasure out of making her say cunt again and again.

Then we had moved on to my body and, finally, I had allowed her to touch me and to grope my cock. But only from behind cloth. When she had tried to undo my trousers, she had earned my ire and got herself another spanking. This had ended our sex session and I was now sipping coffee and she was dressed in a T-shirt and jeans.

'I do not want your father's whole wardrobe,' I said.

'Okay,' she said. 'Take this.'

And she gave me a coupon for five thousand rupees for clothes. I shrugged. I didn't need it, but the girls could do with some clothes. But then I had a flash. I went to the shop and cornered the young manager.

'How much cash will you give me for this?'

He looked at it and shrugged.

'Nothing,' he said.

I realized that there was nothing in it for him, so I waited until someone came up to the counter with a sizeable purchase. Her bill was seven thousand, and she willingly gave me four thousand in cash when I spun her a story about needing it for my mother's ill health.

I walked out of the store with four thousand rupees but with the feeling that this needed to be made simpler. I needed to be able to convert stuff into cash. Or I had to work out a way to make the women pay.

The idea itself was simple. I was offering a service. They were actually hiring me for it. They should pay. But this intersection of commerce and sex made them uneasy. Presumably, they wanted to believe that I wanted them for themselves, maybe even for their minds. They wanted love.

I was not offering love. I was offering sex.

Would I earn more if I pretended that I was in love with them?

This may have been the first time—outside that fancy shop, on my way to the bank, with four thousand rupees in my pocket—that I began to think of this as a career. Up until then, it had simply been a bonus. I was being paid and I was getting my tubes cleared and I was picking up in confidence. I don't think I would have ever thought of speaking to Aparna or taking her to the Taj if it were not for the fact that I had satisfied two mature and upper-class women. On the debit side, I had been scared away from one. By an old woman.

I tried not to think about that. And I tried very hard to conjure up the kind of person who would please Rewa.

You may think it is easy to have a slave, but it actually takes a lot of work. They want you to snarl at them all the time, and if you take some time off they try to do things to irritate you. This is particularly stupid because most of these things are not exciting at all. For instance, I said to Rewa that she should spend the next ten minutes as my footstool, crouched on the floor. I did not particularly want this; what I did want was how wet and ready she would be afterwards. A little humiliation went much further than the endless quantities of foreplay that every other article about sex suggested.

It sometimes disturbed me that she would be weeping as I entered her. It was as if she were sending out two messages at the same time: the first was that she hated me and all that we were doing; the second was that she was enjoying it immensely. I didn't know what to make of it—so I made nothing of it, and continued to enjoy her body for some months.

Meanwhile, Aparna thought I was a real gentleman.

'Thank you,' I said. 'And why is that?'

It was a Sunday evening in April. April is indeed the cruellest month on the pocket of the tutor. There's a small burst of activity at the beginning of the month as the year comes to an end and everyone wants extra time. Then the exams are over and, as we say in my part of the world, 'The fever breaks, the doctor dies.' The family calms down. The child is set free. The holiday, once a distant plan, is now reality. There is shopping to be done and promised treats to be redeemed. Who wants to see a tutor then? Only those who are preparing for the tenth standard, but even these eager beavers want Sundays off.

This means much less money, but it also means more free time. In another era, I would have spent this time reading Fyzee on Muslim law or Salmond on torts, but my dream of practising seemed to be fading fast. When I got angry with a kid for not doing his homework or for not living up to his potential, I did not think: 'What am I doing wasting my time with this boy when I could be working under Pitlawala and Surajmukhi?' Now my anger expressed itself as: 'What am I doing wasting my time with this boy who may do badly and ruin my reputation as someone who can bring home a ninety per cent or above?' It was a shift in who I was. Part of this shift was also due to Aparna.

'It's teaching,' she said earnestly when I disparaged what I did. 'Why do we despise tutors so much and respect teachers so highly?'

I shrugged. I didn't really care. 'Maybe it's because teachers are paid so badly that we try and make up for it by offering them respect?' I suggested.

'And tutors are paid so well that we see them as scum? I don't know. I don't think tutors are even paid that well… are they?'

This was dangerous territory. Why was she asking?

'Why?' I asked lightly. 'Are you afraid I'll stick you with the bill?'

We were sitting on the top floor of Café Naaz, one of the nicest ideas that the city has had. It is perched on Malabar Hill and, in the evening, you can watch as the sun dunks itself in the sea and the lights begin to come on. If you don't remember what it looks like, try *Qurbani* with Feroze Khan and Zeenat Aman. The fight sequence in which Vinod Khanna rescues Zeenat Aman takes place at Naaz.

'No, I was just thinking of the maid who works for us. She has two children and she was telling me that she pays two hundred rupees for their tuition.'

'Where does she live?'

'I don't know. Kandivali, I think.'

'Oh, in the suburbs things are different.'

'Yes, but you know, she pays two hundred rupees and some woman teaches them…'

'Does she come and teach them, or do they go to her?'

'That all I don't know. Why?'

'Makes a difference. If she comes home, then she's their tutor. If they go to her house, they're her tuition pupils.'

'Good grief, what does that mean?'

'It's not just a semantic difference; it's an economic difference. If I am your tutor, you get my services for that hour. It means I only get what you pay me for that hour. If you are my tuition pupil, I charge you a certain amount, but I may also charge others the same amount for the same time.'

'Chhee!'

'Okay. What are their names?'

'Whose names?'

'The names of your maid's kids?'

'I think...no, I've forgotten. Something generic. No wait, the names rhyme. Yeah, that's it. Ajay and Vijay maybe, or Rajan and Sajan?'

'Okay. Let's call them Ajay and Vijay. And let's call their teacher Mrs Pai. If Mrs Pai comes to Ajay and Vijay's house, she is going to teach them alone. And she will get two hundred rupees at the end of the month. If Ajay and Vijay come to Mrs Pai's house, they may find Sujoy and Bijoy also there. Namita and Nirmita may also be there. Each of them will pay two hundred rupees.'

'But that's exactly like a tutorial class?'

'Not really. Classes can have fifty kids in a single room sometimes. Here the maximum will be six or seven.'

'Why? What's to stop her from putting in fifty?'

'Space. Mrs Pai probably lives in the same slum as all her students. She probably has her own kids and her in-laws all living in the same space. How will she put bums on seats if she doesn't have seats?'

'Gosh, it's a business.'

'See? Now you're already seeing Mrs Pai as some kind of parasite of the poor. She is probably just making a living too, trying her best to get out of the slum or chawl or whatever it is. That's why tutors don't get any respect.'

'You seem to have thought all this out,' Aparna said.

Had I? I suppose I had. You get a lot of time to think

while you're in the bus queue or on the bus; less when you're on a motorbike.

And that's when she told me she respected me.

'Because you're willing to wait,' she said. 'You're not trying to get me into bed.'

There seemed to be a faint hint of puzzlement in her voice. Good. Puzzled women are going to spend more time thinking about you. Puzzled women are also a little off-balance.

I smiled. 'You don't know how much it costs.'

She pretended not to understand.

'There's nothing I'd like more than to leap over the table and show you that I'm not a gentleman,' I said. 'But don't worry…'—she wasn't looking worried, though, only mildly intrigued—'I'm not going to try that, much as I'd like to.'

'There is a via media,' she said, and we walked down Marine Drive in the late evening and then we sat by the sea and listened to the waves murmuring against the sand and we kissed and it was something special.

How was it special? I don't know. It felt like I had been eating hotel food for so long that I had forgotten what home food tasted like and someone had cooked me a meal. It felt like love.

My heart swelled up and I noticed clinically that my penis remained unaffected. I was enjoying this so much—the smell of her body, so fragrant and rich with spice; the touch of her hair, raw silk and midnight-black in the light of the stars; the feel of her against me; the suggestions of other textures under the slipperiness of silk, the possibility of roughness of hair, the tension of muscles. I was enjoying it more than I thought I could, but I was not aroused. I was a little annoyed at myself. I should be hot and hard. What if she reached down…?

The improbability of such a thing happening made me want to laugh and I wondered at how many emotions a person can feel all at once. No Indian middle-class girl was going to reach down and feel a man's cock—not during the first few kisses, at any rate. She had to be guided there, and when she got there she would do everything as if under pressure, only for love, because it's her duty, all of the above.

But the idea that she might touch me produced the first sparks and the first sparks are generally all it takes. I was hard in a few seconds and wondered whether I could risk pushing my hips against hers. Except, she was sitting next to me and only with a lot of manoeuvring would this be possible. And since I didn't want to lose the good impression I had created, I decided against it. I would content myself with her mouth and her face and not even reach for a breast.

Of course, as soon as the thought struck, the need began. I wanted to feel her breast and it was only with a great exercise of the will that I could stop myself.

Lesson learnt: stay in the moment. If you start thinking about something, even in a negative sort of way, the mind begins to respond inappropriately.

Eventually, a cop stopped the kissing party, with the usual questions about what we were doing there, how could we be doing such a thing since we looked like we came from good families, why we weren't getting married, whether we knew how much pain we were causing our parents. I kept a steady pressure on Aparna's hand because I had no intention of letting her get mouthy. After all, this was a Bombay cop, and Bombay cops only start moralizing when they smell money slipping out of their hands.

So I apologized profusely and grabbed both his hands and stuffed a hundred-rupee note into them. Aparna was scandalized.

'How could you do that?'

'Why? Did you want to spend the rest of the evening at the police station?'

'Of course not. But I don't see why...'

'Was it your money?'

'No,' she said, but I could sense that this was not the tack to take.

'Did I ask you for a contribution?'

'No.' She didn't say the word so much as let it slip from between her teeth.

I raised an eyebrow. 'So?'

'It's the principle of the thing.'

'Explain that to me,' I said.

'We were doing nothing wrong.'

'To which I added something wrong?'

'I didn't say that.'

'You meant it.'

'I did, okay, I did. But I don't think bribing a cop is right.'

'I don't think getting a woman into trouble with the cops is right either.'

'But how is he going to get me into trouble?'

'If a cop wants to get you into trouble, he can. It doesn't matter to him because he's only doing his job.'

'He's not.'

'Don't give me that why-aren't-they-running-after-real-criminals stuff. There's nothing in the law that says: "This is a real criminal and that's a false one." If you break the law, you're a criminal. And there's always a law about public morality or public decency.'

'I just don't want you doing that again.'

'I won't. And we won't kiss either.'

'That's ridiculous.'

'Can we make out at your place?'

'No. Are you nuts?'

'And we can't make out at my home either because my mother will throw us out. That means we have nowhere to go unless we rent a hotel room.'

'Oh gosh, that would be infra dig.'

I didn't know what that meant, but I guessed it meant something not nice. 'I am glad, however,' I said, 'that you did not issue a nolle prosequi.'

She looked startled. 'You studied law?'

'No,' I said. 'P. G. Wodehouse.'

She giggled and got onto the bike. This time, I could feel her breasts pushing against me. I had never felt them that way before, which told me something about how she sat, told me something about our kissing, told me something about where we were going.

I began to wonder whether I could get myself a room somewhere. We could have some privacy then. One part of me said, 'You can't get a room somewhere without causing yourself financial loss and slowing down the process of buying your own home.' Another part of me said, 'You know what buying a home costs in the city. You will be in your thirties by the time you're sitting in the bank and signing something. And what will be the use then? You will have to get married and settle down.' I knew which part this was. It was my dick talking.

So, when I had my evening bath, I masturbated so that I would stop thinking about another room in which I could teach children for part of the day and fuck women for another part of the day. Of course, it helped that my mother began to ask whether we had seven lakhs in the bank, as if she did not check the numbers almost every other day.

'Why do you need seven lakhs suddenly?'

'Suddenly?' she said. 'Suddenly, you're saying. As if you live in another world.'

If I go out to work, I come home and am received by Mother Number 1. This one is a pleasant person who wants to give me dinner and lay out nicely ironed pyjamas.

If I go out for any other reason, I am received at home by Mother Number 2. This one is a harridan who claims I do nothing, except for those things that make me happy. I once asked her about this and she went into hysterics and said I was calling her Number 2, so I just bear it. The only thing to do is to repeat the question and ignore the shit that gets thrown at you in between.

'Why do you need seven lakhs?' I asked again.

'I need. Yes, I will buy gold for myself. I will go to foreign. I will do this. I will eat in big-big restaurants.'

She had found the bill for the coffee Aparna and I had drunk. You would have thought I had sold one of my sisters into the sex trade. 'Four hundred rupees for two cups of coffee?' she had shrieked. I tried to convince her that a parent of one of my students had taken me out for coffee—which was true, only just not those two cups of coffee—but she was not convinced. 'So why do you have the bill? Surely he should have the bill! So much money wasted. On top, you are now telling lies.' That kind of thing.

I told myself now that I would not respond to her, I would not let her derail her own train of thought. This was difficult because I was beginning to feel the first spurts of rage against the backs of my eyes.

'Why do we need seven lakhs?'

'For Radhika.'

'A dowry?'

I looked beyond her form. Radhika and Anita were both present and correct.

'Dowry means what? You're talking like one journalist. Ek rishta aaya hai.'

I quelled the urge to say: 'And you're talking like a lyricist.'

'And?' I said instead.

'And means what?'

'So why do we need seven lakhs? Is that the dowry amount or is that the full-and-final figure?'

Radhika began to shift about uneasily. 'Bhaiya…'

Mummy turned to her like a cat defending its young. 'Shut up. Rani banke raaj karegi tu,' she said to Radhika. Then she turned to me again. Suddenly, she was all sugar and spice. 'You listen. This is a good offer. The boy is stable. And mature. He will look after her well.'

I knew what that meant. He was old. 'Widower? Divorced?'

Radhika burst into noisy tears.

'He is an innocent divorcee,' said my mother somewhat mystifyingly.

'Means?'

'Means? Everything I should tell? Nothing you will know?'

I thought about it. The term had come into being to describe women who had got married and then been abandoned but without ever having experienced the delights of the conjugal bed—or so their families tried to claim. This generally involved long, complicated stories about the health problems of the groom which had been concealed, but more often than not it was a simple sham. It meant: 'My daughter got married to a man from America, who then went back and filed divorce papers.' What they did not say was that the daughter had had sex with the man. Of course she had. Which man would not exercise his conjugal rights?

I sighed dramatically. 'I cannot manage this much,' I said. 'But if it means so much to you, I will get a loan.'

Radhika began to weep even more noisily. I should have guessed something was wrong then, but I was sick of all this. If the two had been working, I wouldn't have had to give up all my money—and borrow some—in order to pay for the wedding.

'But let the marriage be in May,' I said.

'Why May?'

'Because there are very few tuitions then. Otherwise, in all the running about, I will lose even more money.'

In the night, I heard something that shocked me to my core.

'What will become of us?' It was Anita.

'Means?' Now Radhika was speaking.

'How will it be? The sister of a tuition teacher?'

'Arre, who asks when there is money?'

'Yes,' said Anita. 'But see what they're asking. For an old man. Innocent-shinnocent, I don't care. For a man like that, no one has face to ask. Yet, they're showing face.'

'Don't worry about it. There's a way.'

I didn't hear the rest of it. All I could think was: tuition teacher, tuition teacher, tuition teacher. The bitches were happy to eat that money. Then there was no tuition teacher, tuition teacher. Then there was only this is needed, that is needed, bhaiya, that is also needed, please buy this for me. Not that I grudged them anything because they had been kept out of any thought or understanding of economy at my mother's insistence on keeping them out of harm's way. Not that I grudged anybody anything. But then, to bite the hand that feeds you by saying, 'tuition teacher', as if it were a profession without a pedigree...

The next day, when I came home, I found out what Radhika had meant by saying that there was a way. There was tension in the house when I entered. Mummy was sitting on the floor, the pallu of her sari pressed into her mouth.

'What happened?' I asked Anita.

'Radhika.'

I looked at my mother. She began to cry.

'She has run away,' she said between sobs. 'Ask her. She knows.'

I looked at Anita.

'What I know?' Anita was pretending. She knew.

'What is going on?' I asked. 'Where is Radhika?'

Now Anita began to cry as well.

'That boy...' Mummy burst into sobs again.

'Which boy?'

Anita ran off and locked herself in the bathroom.

'Muslim...' my mother moaned.

Muslim? Radhika had run away with a Muslim?

'I told you…' Mummy began.

'What did you tell me? I told you to send them to work and you said that they would spoil the name of the family. Now what good has come of that? Has she earned any money? No. Has she kept the name of the family? No. So how is this my fault now?'

Mummy started to weep and beat her breast. I couldn't take it, so I stood up and said, 'I'm going to the police.'

At which, my mother got hysterical. 'No police, no police. What will everyone say? How will I show my face to the world?'

I suddenly thought about Panna Mausi talking about the day the police came. 'Then what do you want me to do?'

'Go and find them and bring her back. Bring my daughter back.'

'Sure,' I said. 'Just like that.'

This only caused a fresh storm of tears. I went and knocked on the door of the bathroom.

'Who is this boy?'

'I don't know anything,' Anita shouted shrilly. It was clear from the tone of her voice that she knew a hell of a lot.

'Who is this boy?' I thundered, thumping on the door.

Anita began to cry loudly. I continued to thump, but then the doorbell rang. Mummy got up and began to totter to the door, presumably in the expectation that Radhika would walk in and all would be right again. I pushed her to the sofa and went to the door.

It was Sethi Mausi from next door. She was not a real relative, but when you have lived on top of each other for more than twenty years, some relationship tag has to be given. So, Sethi Mausi.

'Sab khairiyat?' Sethi Mausi was from Lucknow and had never let anyone forget that.

I shrugged and smiled and tried to close the door, but Sethi Mausi was not to be denied. She had already insinuated some of her body, slippery in a housecoat made of synthetic material, into the door. I could not close it without doing her—or the door—some damage. I yielded to the inevitable and let her come in.

'Kya hua, behen?' she asked and settled down near Mummy, with the air of a hungry but well-mannered vulture.

I said there was nothing the matter at the same time that my mother said that the family name had been ruined and our collective nose had been chopped off by my sister.

'Those boys are like that only,' said Sethi Mausi.

'Which boys are like what only?'

'M-type!' whispered Sethi Mausi. This was difficult because there were two M-types who ruled Sethi Mausi's view of the world of villains. One: the members of a parochial group; the other: members of a religious group. A perfect city would have neither M-type.

'Do you know anything about him?'

'Arre, what I'll know? Do I have time to die? How I am going to find out where and what and who? But everyone knows that he is the only educated member of his family. Otherwise, one brother is a loafer type—he can be seen sitting on a charpai near those wood shops. The other is a driver. Three daughters they have. God knows where they will put our Radhika.'

For someone who knew nothing, Sethi Mausi seemed to know almost everything about our in-laws.

Anita came out of the bathroom. And, in the way of these things, they began to compete about the information they had. It would seem that Radhika had met this boy when she had suffered a fall outside a temple. She slipped on a banana peel (Sethi Mausi), no, on a plastic bag filled with food (Anita), and Imraan had helped her to her feet. She had suffered a moch (Sethi Mausi), sprain (Anita), same thing (Mummy), and he had put her on his bike and taken her to a clinic and had sat with her while she was waiting for the doctor. He had told her that he was an engineer (Sethi Mausi), a computer engineer (Anita), same thing, please why didn't anyone ever tell me (Mummy). She had succumbed to his charms (Sethi Mausi), she had had jadu tona done on her in that clinic because she had come home with that black oil and those oils have herbs in them and dead lizards and God only knows what else (Mummy). Then he had met her the next day and the next and everyone had seen them at the shamshaan ghaat (Sethi Mausi)...

'Arre, marey merey dushman, why the shamshaan ghaat?' Mummy, queen of the non sequitur, asked.

I did not explain that it was a long wall that stretched for about five hundred metres and was faced only by the sea. You could sit there and kiss there, and this was when dupattas and pallus came in handy because they could be used to create a little tent within which you could proceed a little further than kissing.

And now the truth began to out. Mummy had known about this all along.

'I showed you the sand,' said Anita. 'But you said she was doing exercise.'

Since I paid for gym memberships for both my sisters, I thought this a particularly silly excuse.

'So where does this boy live?'

I was told where and I sighed a little. It would be necessary for me to go and see. It was not a desirable neighbourhood, but it was not far away.

'What to do now?' said Sethi Mausi, with the delighted air of someone who sees a situation as past redemption.

'Go now,' said my mother.

'Their marriage is simple. The girl has to say kabool and the boy gets to jump. Finished. She is now Ayesha Begum.'

'Maybe she is not. Maybe not yet. You go and talk to her,' Mummy said.

'They all become Ayesha Begum. Even that actress, what was her name? You know, where I go to see Hindi films?'

'Hema Malini,' said Anita.

'Haan, she. She also became Ayesha Begum. I don't know why. It is not even such a good name.'

'Will she listen to me?' I asked. I thought it unlikely, but I went and got my socks and began pulling them on.

'Of course she will listen to you, you are her elder brother.' Mummy was protesting because she felt she had to. I knew there was no point to this. She knew this too. Then I looked at her and realized that she wanted to show that she had some control over her children. She wanted Sethi Mausi to see this too.

An imp made me ask: 'And you are her mother. Are you coming?'

'What will I do there?'

I wanted to say you will cry and weep and make such a fuss that she might even consider coming back.

Sethi Mausi was gleaming. She piped up: 'I feel sick at the smell of so much meat cooking. But, of course, if you need me I can come.' She said this with so much hope that you could tell she wanted me to ask.

I did not ask.

It was now ten-thirty and I wanted nothing more than to have a bath, eat dinner, catch up with the news and go to sleep. Sethi Mausi was probably right. This rescue act was doomed to failure. If Radhika and this boy had planned it well, the marriage would have happened in the early part of the day and the consummation in the evening, and then it would be a done deal. No going back on a broken hymen.

As I walked towards the area that was to be Radhika's new home, I felt the strange beginnings of something akin to relief. Because Radhika had taken herself out of my equation. She did not have to be provided for. A love marriage meant no horse-and-carriage, at least not from the girl's side. Now if only Anita could find love, if only some banana peel/plastic bag full of Udipi restaurant food would…

Of course, life was about to deal me a bouncer.

Mastani Manzil, I had been told, and it was quite apparent which building it was. There was a bunch of boys waiting outside it. I approached slowly, wondering if this was a good idea. Across the road, I saw a police jeep. Okay, if anything happened…

And then one of the figures in the group separated and began to walk towards me. It was as if he expected to be recognized. And then I saw who it was.

'Armaan?' I asked.

'Teacher Saahab,' he said.

'What are you doing here?' I asked, then felt silly.

'I live here,' he said. And then: 'Your sister is upstairs. She is married to him. Better you should go home now and tomorrow morning everyone can talk.'

I was slightly startled by his tone. 'How do you know where my sister is?'

'Because she has just become my bhabhi,' he said.

I stared at him for a moment and then the penny dropped.

The engineer had two brothers. Another figure detached itself. I presumed it to be the other brother, the loafer.

'Teacher Saahab,' said Armaan, indicating me with his chin.

The young man put out his hand. I took it by instinct and shook it. Cheers and whistles broke out from the group of boys behind. By this innocuous and instinctive act, I had signified my consent.

'Tomorrow morning,' I said. 'I will meet you tomorrow morning.'

As I turned to leave, I could see the cops revving up to leave too. It was over.

All I could think on the way home was: 'My brother-in-law is a driver.' And I realized guiltily that I had no business being angry with my sister for thinking of me as a humble tutor. If I did not like her contempt for the idea of a tuition teacher as a brother, why was I feeling embarrassment about having a driver as a brother-in-law?

That walk home made me realize that I cherished my position in the world. I was a teacher. I saw myself as a professional. The rest of the entourage wherever I went were servants. They were the Rajus who were dispensable and replaceable. I was not.

And what made a driver not-a-professional? He was licensed to drive, wasn't he? And his work was as important as mine. No, perhaps more important. If I did not do my job, a child might fail a test or an examination. This might be bad for his morale, but the kid would bounce back.

If Armaan lost his concentration or mistimed something, people would die.

Only, this did not convince me. Because this argument had not convinced the world. We might teach our children the dignity of labour as a concept, but we would never ask them to clean the toilet bowl. That's the job of the jamadarni. Her work may be important, it may even be vital to our health, but she is not paid as if it were. And she is not treated with respect. Children know this and recognize the dignity of labour as another one of the myriad moral hypocrisies we teach them.

So my problem with Armaan as my brother-in-law was not so much that he was a driver as how the world looks at drivers.

Or so I told myself.

My mother refused to go to their house. And she announced that Anita would not go either.

'Are you sure?' I asked.

Anita looked a bit peeved. She wanted to go and see what this mohalla was like. She wanted to see where Radhika had ended up. I thought it might even be good for her to see, but Mummy was determined. I shrugged and went.

The boys were there, hanging around, but without the air of watchful tension they had had last night. I recognized this only in hindsight.

Three floors up. One-room-kitchen. A great noise from the room which collapsed into an even more deafening silence when I appeared at the door. More people than seemed possible. More furniture than seemed probable. Everything attached to something else so it could be rolled up, put away, hooked to the wall. And in the middle of it all, Imraan, who seemed like a nice chap, the kind you see by the dozen on trains and buses, going to work, holding down a job, eloping with someone else's sister. He did not have any of Armaan's good looks or charm, but he seemed dependable, the kind who would always have some money in the bank and a Plan B in his head.

There was a thin old lady in an armchair, wrapped in a series of blankets that gave her frail body some heft. Her eyes were closed and her toothless mouth moved in silent prayer. She opened them when I came in and I caught a flash of real intelligence. She scanned me from head to foot, decided that I was no threat and shrugged expressively, as if to say: 'I have no part in all this.' Then she closed her eyes again.

Imraan broke the odd silence.

'I am sorry about all this,' he said. 'I tried to tell her.'

She was sitting on the floor.

'Radhika?' I said.

'Meherunissa.' Imraan corrected me. 'Her name is now Meherunissa.'

I shrugged. 'Are you happy?' I asked.

She looked up at me and, suddenly, she smiled and I was dazzled. She was happy. For now, at least.

'Where will you live?'

'It is all fixed,' said Imraan. 'I am going to Riyadh. She will follow…'

'Why can't you take her?'

He looked a bit embarrassed. I looked hard to see if this were a fit of coyness.

'I don't have money for two tickets. Otherwise, my employers prefer married men and they want the wife to come too.'

I took out my cheque book. I had carried it with me.

'My sister will leave with you,' I said and wrote out a cheque for what I thought would be a fair amount.

I felt rather grand until I caught Armaan's cynical eyes on me. In retrospect, I wonder if he had managed this. At that time, I didn't know him at all and so I only thought he could see that I was happy to have got away lightly.

Radhika did not leave immediately, of course. She left a month later. During that month, she tried to visit us on two separate occasions, but she came in a burkha and was turned away at the door. Sethi Mausi took her in on one occasion, gave her tea and no doubt plied her with questions. And so, for a while, Sethi Mausi was added to the list of personae non grata at our home.

Meanwhile, my sex life and my love life continued unabated. I told neither Rewa nor Aparna about the events at home. I don't know why. But I should have known that the truth would out.

A month or so after Radhika left for Riyadh, I was with Rewa. She had spent half an hour with her nose buried in my pubic hair; she had become an expert at oral sex, after the usual pleas and pretence of nausea. (I had not yet trained her to swallow—she said that she could not because she was a vegetarian, but I had the feeling that she might overcome that barrier as well.) And then I had taken her 'against her will', biting her neck, slapping her sides, riding her like a horse until both of us were covered in sweat.

I disengaged and went off to have a shower. There is nothing as wonderful as a post-coital shower with someone else's imported soaps and gels with which you can be lavish.

When I came out, Rewa asked if I would like a cup of tea. I marvelled at her ability to turn from whore and sex toy to South Bombay hausfrau in the time it took for me to wash.

I was feeling at peace with the world and unusually magnanimous. 'Sure,' I said.

'So yoo-er sister is marrying to Armaan brother?' she said as she served me a syrup of milk and cardamom and sugar, lightly flavoured with tea.

'Who told you?' I was so shocked that I did not even bother to try and correct her.

Of course, I already knew. Armaan had told her.

He had needed money for the wedding, Rewa said. They had given him a lakh.

I gasped.

'But kharcha must be from your side also?' she said, her eyes glittering.

I thought about the ticket to Riyadh. 'Yes.'

'And they did kharcha?' she asked.

Some instinct for survival warned me. 'Yes,' I said. 'Inter-caste case, no?'

The glitter died.

I looked for Armaan when I went down to the lobby. He was not there, but on the next occasion that I was teaching Aniruddh, I found him downstairs.

'Kamaaya?' I asked. 'Bhai ke shaadi pe?'

He laughed and threw away his cigarette. Again, I was struck by something, a resemblance...

'Ek do baar hi chance milte hai aise,' he said. And then he said, 'Milke kha sakte hai, Teacher Saahab.'

'Matlab?' I asked.

'Plan hai. Sunoge?'

I almost laughed in his face, and then I realized that he was serious.

'Okay,' I said. 'Bataa.'

'Aise nahin, Teacher Saahab. Baithenge. Kahin baithenge aur main sunaoonga.'

My heart sank. Baithenge is almost always code for: 'Let us drink a lot of alcohol and I will tell you about something silly I want to do that requires you to believe in my business acumen and give me some of your money.'

I almost forgot about it for the rest of the week. Then Armaan cornered me on Saturday. He wanted to meet me. When? I suggested that we meet on Sunday. But where?

'Leave that to me,' he said.

I did and was surprised. It was a three-star hotel to which he summoned me the next day. He looked very comfortable, dressed as if he were Imraan-the-engineer instead of Armaan-the-driver. No tight jeans, no ribbed T-shirt. Instead, he was wearing a business shirt and well-tailored trousers. Nothing was on display. He smiled and explained: his brother was the receptionist.

'Another brother?'

'No, no, a cousin brother.'

Then he pointed with his well-shod foot at a suitcase and my heart sank. Surely, this was not…

Armaan laughed. He could see that I was worried it was charas. Or bombs. 'Aisa kuch nahin hai,' he said. 'Open it and see.'

Gingerly, carefully, I opened the suitcase. Inside it, I found a whole bunch of files. Medical files. Lots of medical files. Different names.

'What are these?' I asked.

'Our passport to wealth.' And he outlined his plan.

It was terrifying. And it was simple.

'What do they pay us?' Armaan asked, and from the sound of his voice it seemed as if he had said this to himself again and again. It had the ring of reasoned rhetoric. 'Nothing. And why do they pay us nothing? Because they say they give us when we need. And when do we need? When someone is in hospital. Now someone is not always in hospital.'

I said nothing.

'Now what happens when we say someone is in hospital? They say: "Bring the papers."'

And then I saw the beauty of this thing. The system under which most employees worked was feudal in a new and terrible way. You have a driver. You give him some white clothes to wear. You pay him a pittance. In so doing, you force him to live in a slum. Perhaps he even has another job. When someone falls ill, perhaps because of the kind of living conditions that slums create, you help with that. This 'help' makes you feel magnificent. It makes you sure that you are a good master. It makes you sure that you deserve the loyalty of everyone who has ever served you for a pittance.

'Here are the papers,' Armaan was saying.

'These are all papers that belong to someone. They have names on them. And dates,' I said. 'Won't work.'

He gave me a pitying look. Then he took out a pad. It was an ordinary pad. A writing pad. Only, it said: 'Shanta Polyclinic'.

'This is our mine.'

Slowly it began to dawn on me. 'There is no Shanta Polyclinic.'

'There is no Shanta Polyclinic,' Armaan agreed.

'But there will be on paper,' I said.

'That is where you come in. We need a bank account.'

'A bank account?'

'Yes,' he said. 'They always say: "I will pay the doctor. I will pay the hospital. I will not give you cash." Why do they say that?'

I took this to be rhetorical, but he was waiting for an answer.

'Because they do not trust us?'

'Because they do not trust us,' Armaan repeated. He had a way of doing that. It seemed as if he were agreeing with you, but it also sounded like he was mocking you for even thinking that there might be another answer. 'So now they will trust. Because we can go to them and show the clinic papers. We will copy them out from these files. And we will show them the bills. Which we will make on these pads.'

He looked at me and, suddenly, he turned into another person. He went from being cock of the walk to being a humble driver. Raju.

'Saahab,' he said, picking up one of the files. 'Yeh rahe kaagzaat. Please do not give me one rupee. But please pay these doctors. You can pay by cheque, sir. You can give me a cheque, sir. I don't mind. I don't mind. But please save my family from ruin.'

And then he threw himself at my feet and buried his head in my lap. I reared up and pushed him off. 'Stop it!'

Lying on the carpet, Armaan glittered at me. I could see his rage and his laughter.

'You know what the trick is?' he asked. 'The trick is the bank account. The trick is the papers. They will give. Oh, they will give. And it will go into a bank account. And then it will come out to you and to me.'

I thought it might be time to talk business. 'As they say in Gujarati: "Maara ketla?"' What would I get?

'Idea kiska?' he asked.

I admitted that the idea was his.

'Papers kaun laya?'

I admitted that the papers were his.

'Bank account kaun banayega?'

He was smart. He was now on my side. I would indeed set up the bank account.

'Aur likhega-vikhega kaun?'

I would also be doing the transcription? I didn't think much of that. Perhaps we could get some help with that? Armaan didn't think so. He had clear reasons and he told me what they were.

'One person can keep a secret. So it is said. Two people, can keep it if both benefit from it. That I feel. Three people, and then it is no secret. Unless everyone gets shares, and even then you are not safe. Two people. Two partners. You and me. My idea. Your bank account. My people. Your writing. This is enough.'

And so it was decided that I would set up the bank account, I would do the paperwork and Armaan would work out the details. He explained that he had already told a couple of drivers and cleaners about the possibility of providing them with fake papers. He explained that there were a couple of gamblers who needed money. These were his first targets.

'They must take someone who has died. No one alive.'

'Why not?' I asked.

'Because, then, if someone really falls sick, people will think: "Oh, I did like this, I did like that, I only made them sick, God is punishing me." And then they will go and cry on this one's shoulder, that one's shoulder, and it will all come out.'

It made sense.

I suggested refinements. 'We shall keep a record so no one can come two-three times in one year.'

He thought about that for a bit. He saw the sense of it. He nodded.

'Except if they work with Parsis.'

'Parsis? Because they are mad?'

'Oho, no one is mad-shad when it comes to money, okay? Don't talk like that.'

I was being lectured on political correctness by an eighth-standard-pass driver?

'Don't feel bad, Teacher Saahab. You are my partner now. And you are my saala. And you are the teacher of my children.'

I took this to be a flourish with the wrong tense attached. I thought he meant that I would teach his children. Some hope. And then I realized that he was my brother-in-law and might have a reasonable expectation of some educational help from me. I felt his gaze on me.

'What about Parsi people, then?'

'Because they are having trusts. They don't have to give their own money. They can give money from other people. So we can do them two or three times a year without any problem.'

It was time to talk about money. Armaan sensed this.

'And now for the deal. Thirty per cent will be mine. Ten per cent will be yours. The rest will be theirs,' he said.

I thought about this for a minute.

'No,' I said. 'Twenty per cent will be yours. Twenty per cent will be mine. The rest will be theirs.'

When we had settled on the figures, I suggested a drink. Armaan laughed. 'Teacher Saahab, I am a Mussalman. Na dukkar ka maas, na sharaab ki baas.'

I was rather relieved. I wondered if he could tell.

As we left the room, he said, 'And, Teacher Saahab, you can ask for a loan for your sister ki shaadi. The boss will give you zero interest. Then you put it in fixed deposit for ten per cent interest. You pay him back regularly and make your ten per cent.'

'Is that what you did with your money?' I asked.

He laughed. 'I don't like fixed rates, Teacher Saahab. Mazaa kya hai if you know how much you're going to make?'

'Then what?' I could already smell a deal. Perhaps I could...

'Better you should not know,' he said, and his face closed up.

But I did ask the Jinkses for a loan for my sister's wedding and asked that they cut it from my pay.

I got some letterheads made, and some envelopes. Armaan was all for doing them on a DTP set-up, but I thought we should spend some money and do a good job of it. I got a friend to countersign a current account in the name of Integrated Health Services. The bank clerk who did the paperwork wanted to know more about it, but when I gave him a couple of Gandhis he lost interest and, within the day, I had made my first cash deposit.

When the Jinkses gave me a zero per cent loan for my sister's wedding in cash, it occurred to me that several other families could be similarly tapped. I went to each with the same proposition. I would give them a set of ten post-dated cheques, which they could deposit at regular intervals.

At the end of the week, I had nearly ten lakhs in cash. I deposited these sums in various banks, all in my mother's name. Still slightly in shock over Radhika's wedding, she signed the joint holder forms without asking too many questions.

I was already earning a steady amount from the interest. I wondered if I should lend it out at a higher rate of interest. But Armaan, with whom I had begun to drink a cup of tapri chai every time I went to the Jinkses, said I shouldn't.

Was this the point at which I realized how much I had come to rely on his worldly wisdom? Not that I asked him for advice. I just mentioned the possibility of lending out the money to him, in passing, and waited for his reaction. He was unequivocal.

'Teacher Saahab, you will not be able to do that business.'

'Why not?' I bristled.

'Because you cannot see a woman cry.'

'You can?'

'Forget me. This talk is not about me. This talk is about you. Suppose there is one child who is holding a gold chain and you have to take that gold chain and the child starts crying and says it is his grandmother's aakhri nishaani. What will you do then?'

I shrugged.

'You will not be able to take it. Why will you not be able to take it? Because you do not know that the child has been trained to say like that. Will you be able to take the child the next time and hold him upside down and shake him until he screams?' he asked.

'Why would anyone do that?'

'Why? Because everyone knows that one time you may get away with that. But next time, they have decided, we will take the chain from the child, whether he cries or screams or does hullagulla. The man says: "Where is that aakhri nishaani, maaderchod?" You don't say anything. You can't say anything. Your mother has made you put the chain in your mouth. Then the man picks you up and shakes you and your mouth opens and he tries to keep it open, so you bite him. He screams and lets you go, but there is another man with him. That man steps up and grabs you and holds you upside down and shakes you until you can't breathe, so you scream and the chain falls out and he drops you on the floor. You fall on your head when the man drops you and your ears ring, but when they have left your mother slaps you and she is weeping because her gold chain is gone. There is nothing left now, understand? Nothing left.'

Armaan was looking straight at the ground. He spat out the tea as if it was bitter. I felt cold too, as if I had looked into someone else's head. Then he shrugged, gave me a half-smile and took out a slip of paper. There was a name on it.

'Good for one lakh at least,' he said. 'Get the papers ready, Teacher Saahab.'

'How does he know one lakh?'

'Because he is the guy who updates the bank books as well, Teacher Saahab. He knows who has hidden what and where.'

This sounded reasonable and that evening we met at the hotel, in another room. Armaan startled me with a rubber stamp that said Shanta Polyclinic. He also helped with the writing, although I didn't think he should.

'Why not?' He seemed offended.

'Your letters. They're illiterate.' His handwriting looked like that of a four-year-old girl—all fat, round letters.

'How can letters be illiterate? Only people can be illiterate.'

I shrugged. I opened a couple of files. 'See?' I pointed to the squiggles.

'What do I see? That people write badly? Doctors' handwriting…'

'Haan. Doctors' handwriting. They are busy. They write fast. They don't take time like that. They don't make letters like that.'

He took a couple of files and began to look through them.

'Sahi re,' he said, and his voice was different now—it was that of a child accepting a truth that should have been self-evident. For the first time, he sounded almost respectful.

Armaan turned the sheets he had written over and began to try and write as a doctor might. Only, he wrote too large. I pointed this out.

'What a world we live in,' he said. 'To look like I am a doctor, I must write like a farmer.' And he grinned at me.

I was struck once again at how handsome he was, how his smile brightened his face…and something else, something I couldn't catch. It was as if I had seen him somewhere else.

Later, when we had finished a nice pile of papers, he stretched and said, 'Ek maarenge?'

'I thought you didn't drink?'

'I don't,' he said, and took out a beautiful cigarette case. It was silver, I could tell, and he had had the good sense to let it tarnish. He took out a cigarette with care, as if it were a rare flower whose bloom might be spoilt by too much careless touching. He lit it and a sweet odour came wafting across to me.

'What is it?' I asked as he handed it to me.

He shrugged. 'If you want it, take it. Don't put names on everything.'

I took a long drag and felt precisely nothing. Armaan kicked off his shoes and went to lie down on the bed. I took another drag, then walked over to the bed to hand him the cigarette. The world was very quiet. It was quite quiet. You could quit while it was quite quiet. Qui could quit while Keith is quite quiet?

'I am high,' I thought. But it was nice.

Armaan beckoned from the bed. He had taken off his shirt and was wearing a ribbed banian. I took off my shoes slowly, as if my actions were all premeditated and needed to be scrutinized thoroughly, and then went and lay down beside him. We passed the joint between us.

'How come you're not married?' I asked.

Armaan shrugged. It seemed to be his favourite means of communication. 'When your plate is full, you should not get up,' he said.

This made a great deal of sense to me then, but it seemed completely meaningless about an hour later. I was eating my third chocolate bar when Aparna showed up. We kissed and she licked some of the chocolate off my tongue. I thought it was intensely erotic and gave her a bite of chocolate to eat. Then I made her open her mouth and took it back. We passed it back and forth between us and she giggled.

'If someone had told me I'd be doing this with a guy, I'd have been shocked,' she said.

'Love is funny like that,' I said, and then I could have bitten off my tongue.

That word. That forbidden word. And I had gone and dropped it into the middle of the conversation.

But it was too late. Aparna had heard and she was pushing her body against mine and kissing my face and generally behaving like she or I or both of us had won the Nobel Prize for something or the other.

'I love you too,' she said.

'I can get her into bed right now,' I thought. 'I can take her on my bike to one of those pay-by-the-hour hotels and I can have sex with her right now.' But I was strangely reluctant. Perhaps it was because I liked Aparna and did not want to cheat her. Perhaps it was because I was getting as much sex as I needed and so didn't have to push it. I thought I might test it out, however, and so I slowly ran a finger along the neckline of her kurta. There was no protest. I ran it back even as I kissed her ear and licked behind it, and then let my finger trace the soft, slow swell of her breasts. I was still moving as if through cotton wool, but the feelings were quite exquisite, as if strained and sieved and passed on to me pure, refined. I wanted to weep at how lovely the feeling was. When my finger became constrained by cloth, I decided against further moves. There was no point in clumsiness. There was no point in a lack of beauty.

'It should be beautiful between us,' I said.

Aparna laughed with delight, a tinkling sound in the middle of the traffic, in the rough rasp of retreating tide along the shoreline.

I should have felt bad about all this. I see that now. I should have known that Aparna would not forgive my behaviour, but those two parts of my world were completely separate.

Aparna represented my social life; Rewa was part of my

professional world. That I was having sex with her didn't seem very different from teaching her children. I know it sounds bizarre, but that's what it was.

Rewa and I had now worked out a fairly good relationship. She would give me money, but it was always money I needed. I would point out that my bike needed servicing and that it would cost two thousand rupees. I would say that my sister needed new clothes and that it would cost three thousand rupees. I tried to match the money to the level of service.

But the truth was that I had no heart for it. Rewa wanted to be treated badly; however, there was a limit to what I could do. I thought it would be enough to get her to worship my feet or to leave my dick inside her mouth for ten or fifteen minutes, but it seemed as if I needed to be upping the ante each time we went at it. I tried some research and pushed her head into the toilet bowl and flushed, which made her orgasm intense but almost lost me my erection because when she bucked under me drops of water splashed all over my torso—I did not know whether this was her sweat or the water from the commode.

I also began to see why prostitution was not really a fun profession as I had always thought. When I was growing up, I had always fantasized about being paid to fuck. I thought it would be really cool to be, say, sitting in a bar, and then this amazing woman comes up to you and offers you money to bring her off. I did not have any of the details worked out. In college, we were always being told that you had to stand at the Wilson College bus stop with a handkerchief peeking out of a pocket, and this was a signal to the sexy aunties of the area whose husbands were too busy to service them. I was very tempted to do this, but it sounded like some kind of fantasy. I didn't know how women would be able to spot a handkerchief and check out a young man and decide on whether to sleep with him in the time it took for her to pass a bus stop. And did women really choose that way? Whatever the truth of that rumour, I had found the idea of someone wanting me enough to pay for it incredibly sexy. Now, when I thought of it, I did not feel the usual physical memory of sexual excitement, the faint fluffing out of my penis, the trickle of delight inside my head.

And, truth be told, I wasn't particularly concerned about the money that Rewa gave me. Armaan and I were making a steady income from our side business. He seemed to have a steady supply of people and he seemed to know what we would get.

'Ishwar will ask for fifty thousand, they will give him forty,' he would say.

'Why?'

'He is a relatively new banda in their household, but he is chikna.'

'You mean someone is having a chakkar with him?'

I did not know why I spoke in a different way with him, but I did. Did I do it to make him comfortable? Or to change who I was?

'Arre, everything is not sex. They are an old couple, both are finished with their vaasanas. But old people also like young people to be around. They have an old man in the kitchen who has been there fifty years, his name is Manoj Kaka. They just gave him one lakh to rebuild his kholi in the village. And all this even after he has been named in their will.'

'How do you know all this?'

'The old one was boasting. See, Manoj Kaka is jealous. He does not like that "Munna" gets to do this, gets to do that. He can see that when "Munna" comes into the room the oldies are smiling. He wonders whether they will change their will. So he wants to take it out now only. There was no problem with the kholi in the village, but he managed to take out one lakh, so he told Ishwar. He is an old fool, because now Ishwar is ready to take out also.'

One day, I saw the two of them together and joined them for a cup of tea.

'I am telling him, Teacher Saahab, to listen to me. You tell him.'

I thought about this for a moment. Would I listen to Armaan? I would.

'If it is about duniyadaari,' I said to Ishwar, who seemed to be paying attention to me as if he were willing to follow my advice to the grave, 'you cannot find a better guide.'

Ishwar said, 'Thank you, sir. I will listen to him, sir. Sir, with you as my guide…'

'Oy,' said Armaan, his voice abrasive. 'He is not a pigeon for you to pluck.'

And it dawned on me that Ishwar had been using his stock-in-trade: he had been showing himself as the young and humble man who is willing to listen.

'So what is this about?' I asked as I lit a cigarette and took my first sip of tea.

'What to say? Money has come into the hand and he is saying give it back.' Ishwar sighed.

I raised an eyebrow.

'The oldies gave only thirty thousand rupees,' said Armaan.

I continued to look puzzled. Armaan sighed.

'I am telling this fool to return the money and say nothing.'

I shrugged my shoulders and looked at Ishwar. 'Do as he tells you.'

'If I do not take one lakh out of these people,' said Armaan, 'I will give you thirty thousand rupees of my own money.'

He then outlined the plan. Ishwar was to go back and give the money to his oldies without a word. He was to say: 'I asked you for money and you gave it to me. I am grateful for your help. Here is your money back.'

'Can you say that much without smiling your jalebi smile?' asked Armaan.

'Arre, I am giving money back. I am sending Goddess

Lakshmi home. What source of happiness will make me smile?'

'I will tell you what to say and you say it. I will tell you what to do and you do it,' said Armaan. 'Just follow my orders and you will be washing your backside into gold vessels.'

I thought this rather crude, but the sentiment seemed to appeal to Ishwar. In due course, we made our cut of the money. It was forty thousand—the one lakh had come through.

'How?' I asked Armaan as we lay in bed, smoking. It had become a habit now, this Sunday afternoon marijuana session. I would get the writing done in an hour or so. Armaan did the nursing notes because they could have somewhat girly-curly handwriting. We worked on a couple of sets of medical notes a week and then we relaxed.

'Simple. He goes and returns the money. They are shocked. They say: "Don't you need it?" He says: "My brother is sick. He is dying. Of course I need it. But I do not want it this way." They say: "Are you mad?" He says: "You must be having problems with money. You are like my parents. If you cannot give me the full money, it must be because you do not have it yourselves. I cannot take money from my parents if it hurts them." They say: "No, take it, no take it." But luckily he has the sense to follow my instructions. When they are getting angry, he falls at their feet and says that he actually needs one lakh, but he could not ask them for it because they have just given so much money to Manoj Kaka and how could he ask for one lakh after that and even with fifty thousand nothing will happen and so on and so on. So, the next day, they got the money for him.'

I laughed. 'I feel sorry for them.'

'You do?' Armaan looked at me with something like curiosity. 'Why?'

'They're so easy to con,' I said, but there was something frightening in his eyes.

'Easy to con? Do you know who is easy to con? Ishwar. I can take his panties away from him tomorrow and he won't know.'

'I think you could take mine and I wouldn't know,' I said, trying to calm him down.

'No, I can't do that. You have education. You can take that education and go out into the market and ask for your price. What does Ishwar have? He has his hands. When the old man shits in his bed, you know who cleans it up? Ishwar. When the old woman dribbles on her dried-up tits, you know who cleans it up? Ishwar. When they get up in the middle of the night, Ishwar gets up in the middle of the night. When they are sitting at the table, they tell him bring this, bring that, then they laugh when he does not know what this or that is. Arre, he is a boy from a small pahari village. Where has he seen fork-knife-dish-spoon? But they think he must know. He must know because Manoj Kaka knows. Manoj Kaka has been there how long? Twenty-five, thirty years. He has had time. He knows this goes here, that goes there. He wants his nephew to work in that house, but his nephew is a drunkard, he will not do this, he will not do that. He gets drunk and one day he starts shouting at the old lady when she makes a mess. He gets sacked and who comes in? Ishwar. When the nephew was there, Manoj Kaka made sure the oldies gave him five thousand rupees. When Ishwar came, how much did he get? He gets two thousand rupees. Now tell me, who is easy to con? Is it the buddha-buddhi or is Ishwar?'

'I see what you mean,' I said.

'You cannot see what it means,' Armaan said. 'Because I look into your eyes and I see innocence.'

I felt a flicker of annoyance. This was perhaps going too far.

'One day,' said Armaan, 'I will tell you my story.'

'Why one day?' I asked. 'Tell now.'

'Your girl is not waiting for you?'

I didn't even ask how he knew I had a girl. The driver network was alive and well.

'She's not in town.' It was true. Aparna was in Coorg, on a field trip, with her class.

'My father wanted to do business, but he was an innocent,' Armaan began. 'He helped people and he thought people would help him in his hour of need. Because that is what you need when you start a business. You need people to help you.'

This was familiar territory. I had heard this story a dozen times before from a dozen different sons. Dad was never a failure. He was never just a bad businessman. He had never over-estimated the demand for his product. He had never got his supply chain wrong. He was just a good man who was treated badly. This made it easy to handle. This made your father's failure into a decent story. For a moment, Armaan's mask slipped. He was not the sophisticated worldly-wise man who knew how to milk the system. He was just another boy whose father had let him down.

'When people came to him, he helped them. And then he found he had no money left.'

And so Armaan's father borrowed one lakh rupees, back in the day when one lakh rupees meant something. That too went to the poor and the needy. Or so Armaan said.

'Do you know how you can repay money like that?' Armaan asked.

I shrugged.

'There aren't those many ways,' he said. 'You can sell a kidney, but you rarely get enough money. My cousin brother did that. The dalaal told him that he would get one lakh rupees, cash. But on the morning of the operation, he brought only forty thousand.'

'Why did he agree to go through with it?'

'Because his father grabbed the forty thousand and ran. Then there was no discussion. He went under the knife. When he came out on the other side, they said: "Your kidney was not as good as it should have been. It was a bit this, it was a bit that." So many words, so many descriptions. How can one say anything? He said he would go to the police, but they laughed in his face. In this country, there is no police for Muslims, there is only police against Muslims.'

I didn't know what to say to that. Again, the difference in who he was and who I was yawned between us. I did not think of the police as my friends either, but I did not think that they were actively against me.

'The kidney thing? It's no good. Another person went. Rameshwar, his name was. He was from the bhaiyas down the road. He was picked up at the free dinner thing. You know the place on Cadell Road, where cars stop and they give hundred rupees or thousand rupees or whatever it is, and so many people get fed? One day a car stopped and they took three people away for testing. Gave them lots of food. Took their blood. Took samples. All sent back with hundred-hundred rupees in the pocket. Next day, again. And again. Finally, Rameshwar's turn. He was all right. His kidney was all right too. They took his kidney, gave him fifty thousand rupees. But the patient died anyway and someone got mad. I don't know who it was, but he came in the night, with the kidney in his hand, and he beat Rameshwar to death and stuffed his own kidney into his mouth.'

I did not know whether to believe this story or not. It seemed to have the ring of truth in it, but it also seemed like something out of the tabloids.

'Kidney is one way. Or you can take a bag somewhere. One bag, five thousand rupees. The only problem is: if you get caught, you go to jail. Or worse. One of my friends took a bag. He got on the train and put it on the rack. Then he was standing at the window. Then someone came and put a big bag right on top and my friend's bag burst. The powder began to trickle out. He panicked and jumped from the running train. That's it. Finished. There only. Another one, I heard about this, he was caught and the police did the worst thing to him. They took his bag and shared it among themselves and told him to go home. He knew what would happen if he went home without the bag. He begged them to put him behind bars, but they refused. So he threw himself into the sea. Finished.'

The nasha was coming down slowly. I was re-entering the real world. Armaan took another joint out of his box and lit it. He did not offer it to me, so I took it from his fingers.

'Take it, take it. How else to live in this world?' he asked.

I heard the sound of an invisible Bollywood dialogue writer in his voice, but with every puff of the grass I felt a deeper and deeper sympathy for him. I reached across and patted him on the shoulder. He sighed and nuzzled into my palm. I felt a little strange about this, but once again I was lifted on the wave of sympathetic understanding and let it go, let it go.

'So, do you know what I did, Teacher Saahab? I came to this very hotel, where there was a man who was taking children to the Gulf. For the camel races. It was not hard work, someone had told me. You would be tied to a camel and you had to just stay on and they would pay you and feed you and clothe you and everything.'

I had read about this. What was it? A slave ring, yes, in which Indian children were sold to Dubai and they rode camels. Some of them were bought from beggar parents. And they killed each other, didn't they? Or they became addicts. Or they were killed. Either way, it was something very terrible.

'This man was the dealer, so I came with my cousin, the same one who works in this hotel now. I told this man our story and he said: "Okay, I will buy you. Take off your clothes." My cousin said: "No, this is not why we have come." And the man said: "This is nothing like that, you donkey. This is to take his weight." I did not know what weight had to do with it, but I took off my shirt-pant. I was wearing shorts underneath my pant. Where we had underwear those days? He said: "That also must go." I thought about Ammi and I took that off also.'

'How old were you?'

'Fourteen,' he said. 'Everything was there,' he added and pointed to his crotch. 'And here,' he pointed to his underarms. 'Nothing here yet,' he said, pointing to his chest. 'Or here,' he said pointing to his head and laughing. It was not a pleasant sound.

'What did he do?'

'He? He did nothing. He was examining the maal. There was maal. He asked me: "It stands?" I said yes. He asked me: "It spits?" I didn't even know what he meant, but I said yes. He said: "Do you want to earn lots of money?" I said: "Who does not want to earn lots of money?" He took my maal in his hand and twisted hard. I screamed. "Don't show me how smart you are. Just answer my questions. If you want lots of money, I can show you how to make lots of money. But you will have to do what I tell you.'"

Armaan told me a sordid tale—the kind you hear every day in this city, he said. I had never heard anything like it. No one I knew had ever been asked to massage strange men who came into the city and asked for boys to be sent to their rooms. No one I knew had ever exchanged his anal virginity for money and a gold coin. (This he wore on a chain around his neck; the chain was a gift from another of his clients, a Dubai-return, he said.)

I had no way to respond to any of this. I felt sorry for Armaan and I felt sorry for Radhika or Meherunissa or whatever she called herself now. She had married into a family that had been forced into sex work.

I felt a little sick now.

'Bye, Teacher Saahab,' said Armaan, and his voice was sleepy, as if he were drifting away. 'Next time, if you don't want to know, you shouldn't ask.'

This was unanswerable because one always wanted to know when one did ask; it was only when the answer fell into the realm of the unacceptable that one wished one hadn't asked. However, curiosity has always been my besetting sin and I know that I must live with the consequences.

I thought about saying some of this to Armaan. When I looked back at him, he had closed his eyes and seemed to be falling asleep. And once again there was something in his face that looked familiar.

I do not know when I realized that Armaan had become something of a friend. I did not have many, as the life of a tuition teacher tends to be somewhat solitary. I did know a few other teachers who passed on students they could not or did not want to handle to me, in return for a commission; I reciprocated but did not expect to be paid. I was, after all, the new kid on the block. Once in a while, a teacher might slip me a five-hundred rupee note for a particularly good contact, but I didn't bother much with all that. I now had three sources of income, all of them pretty good.

It did not occur to me that I could up the take from Stream 2. After all, how many times can a man perform? I was having sex about once a week with Rewa, and that seemed adequate. I did not think to ask whether she wanted me to come more often. I wasn't even sure I wanted to go more often. Of course, there were other women in the world, but even when I did think about it I could see that there were many dangers involved. There were times when I had felt, in the past, that a pupil's mother might be flirting a little with me, but I could never be sure. There are many things women want from men and sex isn't always on the list. What if I started something, suggested something, and things went wrong? The woman might scream blue murder, she might let her friends know... There was no saying where it all would end. Which woman would hire a lecher for her teenage daughter? Or even for her son? After all, it would be suspected that she was hiring him for herself.

And then, one day, I was having a bath in Rewa's bathroom and trying to feel clean again after I had spit in her face and made her clean my shoes with her tongue. Rewa was nattering on outside the door about the price of vegetables. I suddenly thought: 'I feel like a husband.' In fact, we had got into something of a rhythm, with her making me a cup of tea and a sandwich before I left for the next lot of tuitions.

'This lady,' she said when she set down a plate of miniature cheese toasties and chai, 'she toh told to me...'

'She told me,' I said.

'She told to you?' Rewa's pretty brow furrowed.

'No, I meant you have to say "She told me", not "She told to me". You can say "She said to me", or you can say "She told me".'

'Why?' she asked. 'Why like that?'

I shrugged.

'This is very funny language,' she said. 'So she said me, "Do you know anyone who will teach English?" I said, "You also want English teacher?" And then I am thinking, "Ofho, what I have said?"'

I thought it pretty funny too. But then it occurred to me that perhaps this lady was indeed looking for someone to teach her English.

'So who is she?'

'I will not tell,' said Rewa. I had to twist her arm—and I am sorry to say that I mean this literally—before she would give me the number. I called almost immediately and was greeted by a soft voice. Her name was Anukriti, her friends called her Anu.

We made a date, sorry, an appointment, for the next week, on Wednesday. That was the day I usually met Rewa. I calculated that I could manage a quickie and then rush over to the new English student.

When I rang Rewa's bell, she opened the door only a crack. 'What are you doing here?' she asked in Hindi.

'Class time,' I said.

'Class-flass,' she said. 'You have another student, go there.'

Then she slammed the door. In the courtyard of the building, I met Armaan. He had a quiet smile for me, an understanding smile.

'Memsahib is now learning aerobics,' he said.

I looked at him carefully.

'Memsahib likes to learn many things,' he said, and there was now a glint in his eyes.

'I have to go,' I said.

'Haan, haan,' he said. 'Run along now.'

I wanted to hit him. I had to remind myself that I did not love Rewa and that I had also been tiring of the mechanical nature of our exchanges. How was one supposed to do something one did not want to? Of course, she was a beautiful woman, and as soon as I saw those pink-berry nipples, set back in her plump breasts, I was ready for anything. I wondered if the aerobics instructor would discover her needs as I had. I wondered if he would be shocked or if he would be delighted. I wondered if he was like Armaan, someone from a slum or a tenement. I even began to wonder if I were getting a little fat. I reached under my shirt and pinched at my side. A roll of new fat greeted me cheerfully. 'Yes, it's your new love handles, sir,' it said. 'Why don't you drive that bike a little more? Why don't you drink some more tea, eat some more cheese sandwiches, take another toke and then gobble three chocolate bars?'

I promised myself that I would go to the gym more often and rang the bell of my new student's house. If a servant opened the door...

It was not a servant. But the woman who opened the door seemed to be of a certain age. To put it plainly, I had not expected someone who was clearly on the wrong side of forty and only a few birthdays short of fifty. She was fighting this gamely. Her hair was dark red and black in almost equal measure and her skin was so well cared for that it had the look of ancient parchment. I decided as I followed her into the living room that I was going to stick to English. No extras.

But, within a few minutes, it was clear that she was looking for some extras. When I sat down on the sofa, she sat next to me instead of across from me. She let her knee brush mine as she leant across the teapoy to pour me some coffee. She explained that her children had left home and that she was bored. (She said 'borudd'.) She wanted to acquire some polish. (She said 'poll-is'.)

I grew tired of this after a while. I reached out and drew one of her dark-red locks into my fingers and stroked it.

'You must learn to love English,' I said.

'I have heard you are a very good teacher,' she replied.

So Rewa had been talking.

'Rewa and I are like that,' she said, and showed me two fingers twined.

I took her hand and gently pulled her fingers apart. 'Now you and I will be like that,' I said, and led her into the bedroom. It was ready for us, the bed turned down and waiting, the incense burning, the lights turned low. So what if Anukriti-call-me-Anu was in her late forties? She was wearing black lace underwear and her body was fit and beautifully ready. Where Rewa had a full pubic bush, Anu was Brazilian-waxed. Her inner thighs were like steel whereas Rewa's were intensely feminine and fit together like rabbits that cohabit.

We had vanilla sex the first time, me on top, she underneath. She seemed very, very ready and intense about enjoying herself. This was useful, even if there was a hint of desperation in it. Whatever I did, she seemed ready to orgasm. I had only to lick her prickly armpit as I had learnt to or nibble my way down her spine and she would be writhing and wriggling like a fish out of water.

But she was also a slave to novelty. Rather, she wanted me to be a slave to her desire for novelty. I could not do anything twice.

'You did that last time,' she said once when I was licking the back of her knees.

'You did that last time to last time,' she said when I slid the blade of my hand between her buttocks. Since I had got this new move from the video parlour, I was annoyed. She was obviously lying. She didn't like it, so she wanted me to feel I wasn't doing what I should.

'Do you keep score?' I asked.

'No, but I pay,' she said.

With Anu, it was clear where we stood and how we were going to go forward. On the first day, she pointed to an envelope she had placed on the dining table and said with a half-smile: 'If this is not enough, then it is not enough. I will not give more, but I will not give less.'

When I went down in the lift, the packet was burning a hole in my pocket. It seemed rather slim, but when I opened it there were ten five-hundred-rupee notes inside. That made me feel a little better, but there was something about Anu's age and her clinical detachment about the whole thing that made me feel sordid.

So I did what I always did in those days when I was feeling a little down. I went off to the bank and checked my balance. It was healthy beyond my belief. I wondered if I should risk playing the stock market, but after a little consideration decided against it. I didn't know what I was doing and I might lose all that I had gained with the work of my hands and my head and my cock. Instead, I decided that it was time to put down a deposit on a home in some far-flung suburb. Even if I never did live there, it could be an investment for the future.

In the course of a week, it was all over.

I went to the Jinkses' home to teach the young ones and was met by Mr Jinks himself. He was wearing a lungi and nothing else. One immense thigh was visible again.

'From tomorrow, you do not come,' he said.

I must have looked startled.

'Yes, you have to give us money. That is maaf. Gurudakshina from my children.'

'May I say goodbye to them?'

I don't even know why I asked. I had no special affection for the two brats and it was likely that Mr Jinks also knew this. But he shrugged. I went and opened the door to their bedroom. They were both in bed, their eyes closed and, suddenly, I knew why Armaan had seemed familiar. Masked in baby fat, softened by youth, here was his face, reflected twice over. It was such a shock that I turned in amazement and said, 'Armaan…' and then tailed off because I did not know how to complete the sentence.

The effect on Mr Jinks was electric. He leapt up from his sofa, galloped across the polished white marble floor and slammed shut the door of the children's bedroom.

'He is also not here. He has gone.'

'Gone?'

'Don't you know? Gone to Dubai.'

I had not seen Armaan for a few days—but gone to Dubai? Why hadn't he told me? Why hadn't he told me about the children?

'These people go to Dubai like you people go to native place,' said Mr Jinks, urging me to the door.

'My fees?' I said.

'You are a full hubshi. You have taken loan. I am saying that is maaf. Still you want your fees?'

I felt a bit foolish.

'Now you go,' said Mr Jinks. 'And don't come. What-what people.'

The door closed in my face.

Later, in the evening, I went to Armaan's house. I had never been there after the first time and Armaan had not seemed to think it necessary either. He was content to meet in the hotel room down the road. The one-room home seemed to have the same number of people as when I had come the last time. The old lady seemed to be in the same position, with the same number of quilts, making the same movements with her mouth as she said her prayers.

'Maaji,' I said.

She opened her eyes.

'Chale gaye,' she said. 'Sab chale gaye.'

And she closed her eyes.

Then she opened her eyes again and said, 'Tum bhi jaao Dubai. Tum jaiso ke liye best place.'

I didn't know what she meant, but I didn't want to find out. I had the curious feeling these days of being made of glass. Anyone who wanted to could look into me and discover my fell purposes.

That night, I woke up from a terrible dream in which I had written everything down and everyone had read what I had written.

The only way to deal with a terrible dream is to make it a reality.

I am making this a reality.

I am writing this in an airport.

I am on my way to Dubai.

What did I do? How come I acted on the advice of an illiterate old woman who pimped out her own son?

You have to understand that I have learnt my lesson. Wisdom does not always come with learning. It comes when life smacks you in the face.

I was already feeling the loss of Armaan. Without him and his contacts in the servant community, there was no more money to be made out of Shanta Polyclinic. I didn't even want to. Without Armaan, I felt exposed, vulnerable. Ishwar had tried to approach me once, but I was brusque. I had nothing to do with anything like that, I told him.

And then it all came apart.

I went to see Anukriti, once again certain that I wanted to break it off.

The house was looking different.

'Spring cleaning?' I asked, wandering around the room. I stopped at a case of fine watches that had been moved around. 'Nice watches.'

'They are my husband's collection,' she said. 'Come and sit down.'

There was tea and cake.

'Nice cake,' I said.

'Eggless,' she said. Like I cared. And then she added: 'It is my birthday today.' Naturally, she said 'birday'.

'Happy birthday.'

'Mere liye gift?' she asked.

I took her hand and put it on my crotch. 'This is your gift.'

As far as cheesy lines go, this had to be one of the worst. As far as gifts go, it might have been much better if I had had an erection, but I couldn't get it up until I saw her body. Her face was too much of a mask, too smooth and too odd for nature. But once I had flipped her over and was biting the back of her neck as I took her doggie-style, this did not matter. What mattered was that I was now buried inside a beautiful body. But today, she insisted on doing it face-to-face.

We were sitting in bed and she was rising and falling on my lap when the door opened and a whole bunch of women rushed into the room, shouting: 'Surprise, surprise! Happy birthday!'

At the head of the bunch, bearing a cake, was Aparna. Behind her was Rewa.

My cock shrivelled.

Anu buried her face first in my shoulder and then, as I shot out of bed, into her pillow.

The women shrieked. I thought I saw Rewa hurry out of the room. I could not swear to it, but she seemed to be smiling.

Aparna said, 'Ma…?'

Then she dropped the cake and turned and fled.

'Please excuse us,' I said, trying for as much dignity as you can when you're naked and a whole bunch of women are ooh-ing and aah-ing around you. They were gone when I had dressed.

I tried to say something to Anukriti, but she was sobbing passionately, her head still buried in the pillow.

Do I regret taking the envelope I found in the usual place? Perhaps. But I couldn't help it. Rewa was not the only face in the crowd that I had recognized. There were other women there too, women whose children I was teaching. They would have to sack me just in order to keep their reputations safe.

Word would spread.

Soon, I was going to be without a job, without any means of earning. I simply telephoned each one of the parents and explained that I would no longer be able to teach their children. I suggested other teachers and did not even bother to check whether they had taken them or not.

I lay in bed at home, trying not to listen to my mother moaning and groaning about the state in which Sethi Mausi had left the steel plates she had lent her last week. My life was finished, and all my mother could bother about was Sethi Mausi's savage use of steel wool. A line came back to me from my college English literature class. 'About suffering they were never wrong, the Old Masters.' The lecturer had shown us a slide of the painting he was on about—in one corner a small splash marked the end of Icarus, but planting and sowing and whatnot just went on.

The phone rang. 'Some girl called Aparna,' Mummy came up to the bed and snapped. My heart lifted, but I decided that I could not talk to her.

Two hours later, Aparna called again. This time, I thought, I should take the call. She said, and I could hear the tears in her voice: 'Mom killed herself. Thank you.' Then she hung up.

I tried calling her back, but the call kept ringing out. I dialled again and again. Finally, Aparna picked up the phone.

Her voice was cold and dry. 'If you ever try to contact me again, I will let the police know that you were an accessory.'

I tried to laugh this off, but I kept thinking of that model who had killed herself. Her boyfriend had been dragged to the police station again and again. Maybe he had even appeared in court. I couldn't recall. But as far as I could remember, his crime seemed to have been that they were a couple and she had killed herself.

This could happen to me.

The next morning, I made a down payment on a house in Vasai. I put it in Mummy's name and emptied my bank account.

I tried to get back to the law. I went to the USIS library and tried to work. When I came home, there was a blue envelope from one Meherunnissa Sheikh. It was my sister, of course.

'Armaan bhaiya is working in a hotel as a masseur. He is very busy and is enjoying Dubai too much. He says you should also come here. He says you can stay in his room.'

Within the week, I was buying my ticket. I was going to Dubai. I was going to start again.

There must be children in Dubai who need coaching.

And those children will have mothers.

This time, I will lock the bedroom door.

Coming soon…

CONFESSIONS OF
A CALL CENTRE WORKER

KRIS YONZONE

A small-town boy moves to the big city to get away from a government-job-obsessed family and realize his dreams. He joins a call centre to make money—and finds himself turning into just one of the many unknown nightshift workers of India.

After clearing round after round of interviews with managers and assessors from every ass-monkey department they had, I was finally selected to work for Big Blue as a technical support agent (whatever the fuck that was). The less unfortunate slunk back into whatever holes they crawled out from, to the victor went the spoils. On the bus journey back to my rat hole of a flat, while being assaulted by the unwashed armpits of India, I remember being distinctly happy to have a job with a multinational, even if it was a call centre. It was only later, much later, that I realized that taking calls for a living is frowned upon in India—the funny stares I got from people made me feel like maybe I would be better off shovelling some ripe cow dung.

May 2013

Coming soon…

CONFESSIONS OF
A PAGE 3 REPORTER

MEGHA MALHOTRA

An ambitious and attractive girl lands herself a job as a Page 3 journalist with a leading daily in New Delhi. The glamour has her friends in thrall, but the vicious politicking is not what journalism school had prepared her for.

We journalists make for an interesting breed, you know? Nowhere else will you find people so happy to get together and bitch their heads off about the profession they chose to be in. Too little pay, punishing hours, overbearing know-it-all colleagues—all of this to bring you ignorant masses education and entertainment! If we are not the unsung soldiers of this world then who is? It's only the perks which keep us Page 3 journalists tied to our jobs. For, who wouldn't kill to attend a Fatboy Slim concert for free, that too VIP/Press seating? Who wouldn't want go in for a chit-chat with the visiting celeb from B-town? And even if you are truly evolved and care little for cheap thrills, you will surely not be indifferent to those fancy wine-tasting dos you get to review. But, to get ahead, you have to 'compromise'…

June 2013

CONFESSIONS
OF A
Private Tutor

CONFESSIONS
OF A
Private Tutor

VIKRAM MATHUR

RUPA

Published by
Rupa Publications India Pvt. Ltd 2013
7/16, Ansari Road, Daryaganj
New Delhi 110002

Sales centres:
Allahabad Bengaluru Chennai
Hyderabad Jaipur Kathmandu
Kolkata Mumbai

ISBN: 978-81-291-2394-7

10 9 8 7 6 5 4 3 2 1

Typeset in Adobe Garamond 12/16 by Jojy Philip, New Delhi.

Printed at Thomson Press India Ltd, Faridabad.

To Amrita

For something that ended so badly, it began without fanfare, in a house with a view of the Arabian Sea.

The boy I was supposed to teach was a spoilt brat, but I was used to that. As long as they weren't rude to me, I didn't care. I didn't even particularly care if they grew to like mathematics. I just wanted them to pass. If they did better—such is the nature of the beast—they got addicted to success and, without knowing it, without even wanting to, they began to work harder. If they didn't do better at mathematics, I got sacked, but there was always a waiting list of students and another kid and another home and another way of making tea.

Pralay Jha was not doing well and his mother asked, through one of his elder sisters, if we could have a conference.

I should have suspected trouble the moment she used the word 'conference'. Most parents would just come into the room in the middle of the lesson and park their butts in another chair and ask you why their sons and heirs (or daughters and chattels) were not doing well. To which, the time-honoured response works well enough: 'S/he could do much better, but s/he must decide that s/he wants to.'

This one wanted a conference. Perhaps it was just the sister's word. She had probably heard it in an American film and wanted to use it.

'We cannot talk in the middle of this chaos,' said Mrs Jha. Chaos? We were sitting in a room large enough to take in my entire home. There were two of us here, while at home there were always at least two people in my field of vision. To me this was the peace and quiet of an oasis in the desert, but I held my tongue. 'I'll take you to coffee at the Taj.'

The Taj? Wow. I had never been taken to the Taj, only walked through it a couple of times when my parents had taken us to see our relatives in Colaba.

'Wear a nice shirt,' she said and threw me a smile over her shoulder. It was the kind of smile that said: 'You have been looking at my body'.

I had not. I swear I had not. Most of the kids I taught were pretty fucked up. Their parents were absent or cold or unforgiving, sometimes all of the above. I could see how these kids worked hard for love, how they were broken by the conditions that were placed upon the receiving of it, how they went from perfectly ordinary children to monsters and then were blamed for it. I didn't want to contribute to their fucked-up-ness, so I left my libido with my shoes at the door.

This is not as difficult as it seems, except when you meet a flirtatious young fifteen-year-old... But I'm getting ahead of myself. Let's just start at the very beginning, the very best place to start, as Maria soon-to-be-von-Trapp sang.

I didn't have too many good shirts. Just two. One was for parties with friends and the other was for this kind of event, the date, the social outing. I was aware, even as I put it on, that it was now about three years old and that it had begun to look a little tired. The patches under the arms were rough and the last button had been replaced by one of my sisters with a button of another colour. But at least the body underneath it was in good shape. We didn't bother about six-packs then; we thought about shoulders and arms. My shoulders were good, my arms bulged. Vincy, my gym sir, had said once: 'Pay attention to your triceps, and your biceps will look after themselves.' It was good advice. For some reason, your triceps work better at swelling out the sleeve of your shirt than your biceps. Perhaps it's because your arm is at rest against your side more often than your elbow is bent up against your upper arm. And I knew that my calves and thighs were fit to be seen. All that walking, from home to home, up the slope of Pedder Road, down the slant of Malabar Hill, up the steps, down the steps. Every day, I logged several kilometres in the Millionaire Mile between Mahalaxmi Temple at one end and Walkeshwar at the other. The distances were too short for taxis to be willing to come; the wait for buses was too long. Yes, my legs were in good shape. You couldn't bounce a coin off my glutes, but why would you want to?

I arrived at the Jha home at 11 a.m., as instructed.

'Would you care to go out?' Mrs Jha asked. 'Or we could stay at home and be comfortable.'

I was so raw, I didn't even think this one through.

'You did say coffee at the Taj?' I said.

She looked at me for one long moment and then said, 'Then coffee at the Taj it shall be.' She smiled, once again with a glint of mischief. 'I try not to disappoint.'

'I'm sure you don't,' I said, which was a foolish thing to say. Nothing much as a comeback, but it was the best I could do at that point because I was looking at her with new eyes.

I didn't know much about her. I knew her name was Prema and that she had been widowed several years ago. She had two daughters, both gorgeous, both very different from each other and from her. I had studiously avoided looking at these two young women, although they often sauntered through the room, leaving it full of rich woman smells.

I should say that Pralay was a late joinee. I inherited him from Pandey Sir, who had shifted his base to the north of Mumbai after retiring from a school in the Millionaire Mile. I paid him a thousand rupees for the referral, but the only time I could make for Pralay was at seven-thirty in the morning. He would be up and ready in his school whites, but the college-going elder sisters would be just drifting into the dining room where we were studying, ripe with sleep. I remember a moment when one of them took a long, deep angdaai, and her beautiful breasts pushed up against the chenille of her nightgown. (Was it chenille?) It was the next morning when I used the image while I was masturbating as I soaped myself during my bath. That self-pleasing quickie was the highlight of my day; it helped me keep my libido in check and it kept me in touch with my sexual self. For the rest of the day, my penis lay inside my Y-fronts, quiescent and taking the air only when I needed a pee.

Mrs Jha had never surfaced during these morning sessions. She was a late riser and there was an elderly aunt who loved getting Pralay ready for school. 'What to tell you, sir? I have to bathe him myself,' she said to me once. The twelve-year-old boy blushed brightly. I looked away quickly, pretending not to have noticed. If the old woman was getting her jollies by bathing this young man, if the young man was getting his jollies by being bathed by the old woman, who was I to interfere? But, of course, you can't confess without there being a fallout—the next time I went, the old lady was looking rocky and Pralay was looking sulky.

'What happened?' I asked Panna Mausi.

'Oh, he is all grown up now,' said Panna Mausi with a break in her voice. 'He does not need his mausi.'

'Oh, shut up,' Pralay said, but it was a plea—you could

tell. He drew out the 'up' so that it had three syllables and two tones.

'See how he talks!' said Panna Mausi. 'I am telling you, it is kalyug.'

I swear. She did say it. I never know whether it is Hindi films which write the dialogue for people's lives or people's speech patterns that determine Hindi film dialogue. I suppose there's a give-and-take.

'What did he do?' I asked.

'Nothing,' said Pralay sulkily

'Nothing,' said Panna Mausi tragically.

'I am twelve years old now,' said Pralay. 'I can take my own bath.'

'Sure you can,' I said. I felt bad for the old lady, but she had done herself in. I am sure that Pralay would have let her continue bathing him until his first pubic hair appeared if she had kept her mouth shut. But since she had needed to confess, he had had to cut her off.

That was perhaps the first time I realized that it was the House of Bernarda Alba. There was no masculine energy anywhere at all. Even the servants were women: tough, hard-working women from the villages, women who could carry a trunk on their backs and climb stools to pull heavy things off the tops of cupboards. Women with bodies so hard that you might mistake them for tree trunks, but women still. Pralay was the only man, but we know, don't we, that we all begin as women? The basic embryo is female until a burst of androgen turns it male. Again, once you're out of the womb, you spend your babyhood as a baby. Proud parents may say that they can see how sweetly feminine Gina-aged-six-months is or how macho and demanding Sohail-aged-seven-months is, but actually babies are babies. They are machines for eating and shitting and throwing up and sleeping. That's about it. Masculinity comes into play only with puberty.

And into this house of women without men I had walked.

Hmm.

Coffee at the Taj? I wanted to kick myself as I walked down the corridor to the lift, following the swing of that cute little tush in the tightly wrapped sari. I was looking at Prema's body now, and I realized that she was in great shape. She either took a great deal of care of it or she was naturally blessed. Her body had a curious golden hue, which she had imparted generously to her three children. And her hair was a nice thick rope down her back, not too much of it, not too little.

When we were ensconced in a bay window at the Taj's coffee shop, I took a careful look at her face. Wide forehead, nice eyebrows not picked too fine. Some laugh lines on either side of her eyes, a lovely brown, the colour of old amber. (Is there such a thing as new amber?) Her jaw was firm still and her neck was good. But her breasts—her breasts were truly magnificent. She let me have a look at them, dropping her pallu as she leant over the table to pick up a menu, and artlessly, so artlessly, she left it lying like a serpent across her stomach. The menu she held on her lap so that I could continue to look.

'How old are you?' I blurted out.

She looked at me for a moment. Then she dropped the menu and deliberately rearranged her pallu, bringing it studiously across her shoulders.

'Don't you know you should never ask a woman her age?' she said, continuing to maintain eye contact.

Was it the eye contact? Was it the sultry contralto? Was it the smell of jasmine wafting across the table? What was it about this innocuous remark that turned it into a catalyst? Why was I erect and aching? Why did I want to leap across the table and rip her blouse open and bury my face in between those lovely fragrant mounds of flesh? How much would they give? How much would they resist?

At one level, at an ordinary, rational level, I knew why I was reacting like this. I was a starving man in front of a feast.

I should explain.

When I joined college, I knew two things. I wanted to be a lawyer and I wanted to have money with which to get women into bed. I was, as most men at eighteen are, socialized enough to know that you couldn't do this just like that. You didn't get to have sex just because you liked a girl in your class and she liked you. You had to invite her out. She had to accept. You had to impress her. And this took money. I had some pocket money from my father, but he was the kind of man who didn't think anyone should have sex with anyone else until they were married, so he didn't factor that into my pocket money. He calculated my bus fare to college and added a hundred rupees a month as emergency money, just in case I needed to come home by taxi. If I spent any of my emergency money, I had to explain why or repay him. In three months' time, I was in debt and the fights were getting regular.

That's when I decided that I would give tuitions in mathematics. It is a subject I know. It is also a subject which has a steady demand. I didn't know at that point if I could teach it, but I did know that there was a market. Three years later, I was doing pretty well at it. I made enough money to bribe and seduce and impress a girl—I shall call her Sunayana and beg her pardon should she be reading this—so much that she actually allowed me to lick her cunt.

We were in her parents' bed at the time since they were away for the weekend. We had been kissing for hours, so my lips were dry and hers were beginning to hurt. Her breasts, she complained, were feeling like atta, with all the squeezing and rubbing that I had done. I bent down to kiss them, but she just pushed me wordlessly on. I worked my way down, past her stomach, her beautiful mound of a stomach, to the rough fur of her mons veneris. I tried to pull her skirt down, but she would not let me. I reached under it and found to my surprise and delight that she did let me. I pulled her panties off and began to explore her hair. At that moment, I came, firing repeatedly inside my pants, unable to control myself. My fingers dug into her and she yelped.

'Sorry,' I said. 'Sorry. Let me kiss it better.'

And before she could do a thing, I had burrowed under her skirt and pressed my face onto her. Of course, I knew I was near the destiny of my delight, but I didn't know its topography very well. Somewhere here, somewhere here. And then my angel guided me. Her fingers on either side of my head drew me to the sweet spot. Here was honey and lemon and fire. Here was my heart's desire. Here was a strange smell, so warm, so human, so woman. Here was hair and then, in the middle of it, a pink and brown nubbin, so intimate, so coy. I wanted to consume her. I wanted to snarl and snap and rip. Instead, I put out my tongue and touched her clit. It was a beautiful moment and I was ready again, my cock pushing against my pants, the orgasm I had just had forgotten except for a faint discomfort along the edges.

What would have happened that day? If Malti-the-maid had fallen and sprained her ankle and been unable to get to work? But Malti was surefooted and she arrived in the house and my angel was expelling me from paradise. However, I knew I was on my way.

And then my father threw a spanner into the works.

He died.

He died and, suddenly, I realized why he had fought me over every hundred-rupee note. We were a subsistence economy. We lived, the five of us, on his salary. He got it, we ate it. There was nothing in the bank. There was no money anywhere. And now my tuition money had to run the house.

I got to work. I increased the number of hours I was working. I increased the frequency of my visits. I raised my rates. And, within two months, I was handling the entire economy and managing to put away some money too.

But this meant the end of the relationship with Sunayana. She was a girl from a big house, as the saying goes, and she had the tastes that went with such a pedigree. Not for her coffee by the yard at an Udipi restaurant, oh no. It had to be an air-conditioned restaurant. Not for her a bunch of flowers created out of a walk through Malabar Hill, oh no. It had to be a glacial bouquet whose exotic qualities were emphasized by the cellophane wrapping and the curlicues of ribbon at its base. This should tell you that I tried these variants when I was trying to get back into the pairidaeza of her thighs. Didn't work. She went on a holiday to the USA, a long holiday, so long that when she returned she had a new wardrobe, a new nose and a ring on her finger.

After that, I threw myself into my work. Not because of a broken heart but because of my mother. She had always been a quiet figure in our house because she had not been allowed to talk much by my father. If she said anything at all, he would say, 'Go out and earn and then you can talk.' This was unfair because she was a tenth-standard pass and he had prevented her from studying further or working at anything. Incarcerated at home, she had forgotten what little English she had learnt. You might think this would have made her eager to make her daughters independent, but it didn't. She wanted them to be carbon copies of herself. She allowed them to get their degrees, but even while they were studying they were expected to come home immediately after classes were over. There were to be no extracurricular activities, no part-time work, nothing.

'Let them also work,' I said often. 'Let them contribute.'

Immediately, Mummy would turn on the tap. Your father would not have wanted them to work. Your father would not have allowed them to work. Your father would not have compromised their dignity.

After a couple of scenes like this, I decided that I would just have to earn their dowries and get rid of them. More work. More tuitions. From Pralay at seven-thirty in the morning right up to Moyna at nine-thirty in the evening, Sundays included, one hundred rupees an hour, all tax free. It added up, but not fast enough.

So I had had no time for romance. I was out of touch. I did not know how to talk to women unless they were mothers or elder sisters or mausis or chachis or phuphis or something like that.

'I'm sorry,' I mumbled at Prema. 'It's just that you look so young.'

She laughed, and suddenly I felt her knee touch mine under the table. You will think I am a duffer, but I moved mine away thinking it was a mistake. However, she was kind—or she was desperate. She moved hers back and this time she looked at me as she applied a deliberate and delicate pressure against my knee. My cock almost jumped out of my pants to salute her.

'Tell me about Pralay,' she said.

'Pralay?' I said. I almost added 'Pralay who?' but managed not to say it. Instead, I said the usual things I say: 'Pralay is a very bright boy. He can do very well if he chooses to. But he must choose to. I can only give him the tools.'

'I can imagine,' she said and bit her lower lip so quickly that I would never have been able to swear whether she had done it or I had imagined it.

But even if that fleeting expression had not crossed her face, even if it had only been me seeing what I wanted to see, by now I was sure. Mrs Jha was flirting with me. I did not know what to make of this, but I was intoxicated. I wanted her more than I had ever wanted Sunayana. I wanted her more than I wanted my sisters to get married and move out of the house. I wanted her more than I wanted to take my mother on a trip to that city in the north and discover that she wanted to stay behind, a corpse-throw away from the great river. But I also knew that she was my employer. She would set the rules of play. It was her game.

'So, you know what they say about taking a horse to water, but not being able to make it drink?' I said.

She nodded seriously. 'I have no problem with that. You are good for him. He needs a man in the house.'

I smiled.

'I do too,' she said.

I was beginning to feel my groove come back.

'Surely that shouldn't be a problem. A beautiful woman like you.'

She laughed. 'But, you see, I am beginning to think that I am not using my mind. I would like to take lessons in French.'

'Yes, that's a good idea. The Alliance Francaise…'

'I would like to take lessons from you.'

Then it dawned on me. From where I was standing, she was a rich woman, a free woman, who could live her life as she pleased. But she probably wasn't. She had to manufacture a reason for us to meet.

'Shall we start right away?'

'No, not today. This is the time when the house is empty. Mausi goes to the temple and Nita goes with her. The kids are in school or college, so we can do lessons without interruption.'

Nita was probably the maid, one of those women with the tree-trunk bodies and the rock faces, who looked like they had been born to be drudges. Eleven o'clock suited me as well. It was the time when everyone was in school, whether they had morning shift or afternoon shift or nine-to-four timings. It was generally the time that I spent sitting in the USIS library, trying to get serious about a law degree that I was doing part-time.

'Okay. Tomorrow?'

'Yes, tomorrow will be good.'

We finished our tea and for the first time in my life I ate

Taj ka khaana—but I cannot remember any of it. I don't know what they put in front of me; I ate it all without tasting a thing.

Outside, in the sea air, now warm against our faces, she said, 'What do you eat for breakfast?'

'Jo bhi,' I said.

'Non-veg?'

'Sometimes.'

'Please don't eat non-veg tomorrow morning,' she said. 'Can I drop you somewhere?'

She was again my employer. I tried to let my arm rest against hers in the car, but she withdrew it studiously. This was going to be a risky business. That added a certain zest to it—as if any more were needed.

The next morning, I debated masturbation seriously before I went in for my bath. I did not want to embarrass myself the way I had with Sunayana. My recovery time would have probably saved the day if Malti-the-maid had not destroyed it, but I didn't think I was going to be able to do the same this time. So, although my cock was hard—it had been hard through the night—I only washed it carefully and soaped my pubic hair three or four times.

It was warm when I stepped out and I hoped I wasn't going to sweat. Of course, if you hope that you aren't going to sweat you become aware of every drop, and each drop adds to your certainty that you are smelling terrible. I spend a huge amount of time in the sun. This means that I sweat. Because I am human. But I had learnt to carry a can of deodorant with me to mask the smell of my humanity. And so, in the middle of a pleasant daydream in which Prema Jha's silky black hair was caressing my hips as she brought her ruby-red lips down to my cock, I imagined her wrinkling her nose in disgust at the smell and withdrawing. I went to the bathroom and sprayed the deodorant into my pubic hair.

I almost screamed aloud. Only the thought of the child sitting a few feet away in his bedroom, waiting for me to come out and assign him homework, stopped me. My entire pubic region was on fire. The deodorant was stinging madly. I had grown accustomed to the burning sensation when I sprayed my armpits; I had not bargained for the fact that the skin below the belt had not been sprayed like that before.

My hard-on, which had not subsided for the last twenty-four hours, vanished magically. For once, I could tuck my three back into my underwear without having to wiggle and pray that nothing was going to go wrong.

At the Jha residence, at 11 a.m. sharp, Prema opened the door for me. I went inside and turned towards the dining room where I normally taught Pralay.

'Nah,' she said, cutting the word off at the end. 'This way.'

And I stepped into her bedroom.

It was an odd room. The floor was marble, but the bed was a cot. It was covered with a couple of plain rough sheets. There was a cupboard from which the mirror had been removed.

'A widow's world,' she said. She seemed to be watching me. 'Welcome.'

'You can't be serious,' I said.

'I am. This is how I live.'

Then she walked into my arms and I was kissing her violently, possessively.

'Arre,' she said 'Slow down. You cannot leave marks.'

'I don't see how that is possible,' I said. This was getting easier. 'Your skin is like a peach.'

'You fool.' She laughed. 'You can't leave marks where they will show.'

I bent down to kiss her neck.

'Never the neck,' she said. 'The neck is always difficult to explain.'

I lifted the weight of her black hair, which had not been twisted into a plait and hung down her back. I kissed her on the nape of her neck.

'Not here,' I said. 'Here I can do what I want.'

She moved a little in my embrace and I learnt over the next few weeks that this was how she showed her approval of what I was doing. She would not moan aloud; she had schooled herself not to. She was one of those strong, silent women.

This also meant that she set the pace. She knew how much time we had and she wanted to make the best use of it. So she brought my head back to her mouth and began to fiddle with the buttons of my shirt. I took it off quickly and then began to fumble with the hooks of her blouse. She slipped out of it and, suddenly, I was in possession of her breasts. They were beautiful, full, pliant, gorgeous. Most of all, what was beautiful about them was that they were real. They had not been photographed by someone else and printed by someone else. They had not been invented in the middle of my bath. They were here, they were real, they were mine. I could do with them what I wanted because they would be covered again by cloth and so would be safe. (Later, I would discover the uses of a needle in a situation such as a love bite.)

'Are you going to look at me all day?' she asked and began to twist her thighs together.

I moved quickly, almost falling out of my clothes.

'The condom?' she asked, and I could have screamed my frustration aloud.

I had forgotten about the condom. And it was obviously my responsibility. Mine alone. A woman in her position could scarcely be expected to go out and buy condoms. No woman could.

'Shit,' I said.

'Never mind,' she said. 'There are still some things we can do without one.'

I could have kicked myself. She was going to give me a handjob and send me on my way. But when we lay down on the cool floor, she began by kissing my shoulders and licking her way down into my chest hair. She nipped at my nipples, startling a yip from me.

'But make sure you don't do that to me,' she said with a mock-warning. 'I am very sensitive there.'

I took her seriously, not knowing that it was her way of asking me to do precisely that. I had a lot to learn about the ways of women.

She kissed me languorously and long and once or twice my body bucked so much that I thought I was going to come. My dick was leaking madly—pre-cum, thank the stars. And then she raised her body away from mine and lay back on the floor.

'My turn,' she said, and I rose to the occasion. I made sure I kept the lower half of my body away from hers because I did not trust myself to let my body touch hers—I might go off like a shot.

Finally, when I was licking her clit, there was a moment of surcease. She began to thresh about, she began to buck her hips, and when I made bold to suck deeply of her inner thigh, she came in an unmistakable manner.

It is impossible to explain how magnificent I felt at that moment. I was on top of the world. I had conquered Mount Everest. I had run a four-minute mile. I had won a Nobel Prize in fucking.

When she lay limp beside me, she reached for my organ.

'Never mind,' I said. 'Not today.'

And I watched with delight as a line of confusion marked

her brow. The delight expanded to include superiority. I had brought her to orgasm and I had left her dazed. I slipped out of the house after a quick wash.

The next day was a Pralay session. He handed me an envelope. Inside it were ten hundred-rupee notes.

I had been paid.

I had been paid for sex.

I had been paid well for sex.

I had never used a prostitute—sex worker, I should say—but I remember crossing the Oval Maidan late one night and being accosted by one. 'Hand mosan ka paanch rupaiya. Moonh mein dus rupaiya,' she had said. A handjob for five rupees had seemed like a good deal, except that I had caught a glimpse of her face and lost any desire to be serviced by her. She was well past her prime and had painted her face as if she were a clown: red daubs on her cheeks, blue eyeshadow and black streaks near her eyes.

I was now her brother under the skin.

I should have felt bad about this, but I didn't. I felt magnificent. It would go, I told myself with a chuckle, towards the dowries of my sisters. It was not for me, it was for them. I even laughed a little at my own hypocrisy.

Late that evening, I got a telephone call. It was Prema Jha.

'Can we have another French lesson next week?' she asked.

The house was quiet around me. All my family was asleep.

'Yes,' I said. 'This time we can start with a French letter.'

She didn't get the joke. She didn't have to. I did.

I wish I could say that I performed as well again, but I should have known that pride goeth before a fall. (Not that I have ever understood that. Surely pride goeth after the fall?) As soon as I arrived with my hard-won pack of condoms—this was in the time of Nirodh, when going into a chemist's shop to ask for a prophylactic was like shouting 'I'm having sex! I'm having sex!' and aunties would crane their heads around uncles to look at who the besharam behaya jaanwar was—we were at it. I almost tore Prema's blouse, but she didn't seem to mind. She was an inventive lover. One of the defining moments for me was when she raised my arm and began to lick my armpit.

I had no idea that the armpit could be so erogenous. I had no idea that there was a direct nervous connection between my groin and my armpit. I had no idea that a woman could lick so lovingly and just when I had got used to this, inasmuch as anyone can get used to the sensation of having one's cock tickled from within, she opened her mouth and took the fleshy bulb in and bit down, gently but firmly. I moaned so loudly that she had no option but to raise her body and suppress the sounds of my pleasure with one of her ample breasts.

I want here to think about her nipples. They were beautiful and pink. I have always felt a great enjoyment of the colour of nipples. They are so various and beautiful that when I am at a bus stop or a train station I spend my time assigning colours and shapes to the nipples of the women passing by. Hers must be pink and tiny, almost hidden in the yellow-whiteness of her breast. Hers are dark, almost black, and the areolae must be large and diffuse. I bless this breast with a pert mole at the corner of the breast and wonder at the magnificence of construction of these two. I look at the shapely and the shapeless and I think about their nipples.

Prema's were, as I have said, beautiful and pink. The nipples themselves had given in to the demands of time and the imperatives of three urgent mouths sucking at them. Three? Surely her husband must have feasted too? He made four. And then there was me, five. But this did not matter to me. I loved the random bumps and contours of her multinipples and the way the areolae grew flushed and hot under the demands of my mouth, as they bore bravely the impertinences of my tongue and the abrasion of my teeth. I loved the way there was no real demarcation between nipple and breast, just a fading away of the roseate hue, from ashes-of-roses to salmon-pink to flesh.

It was all too much for me, this investigation of my body, the way she had of making her body into a worshipping of mine. I entered her and my heart sang and the blood thundered in my ears. This was conquest. This was her surrender. This was my blooding. This was how I was to enter the ranks of men.

You never forget your first pay packet. You never forget your first fuck. I learnt that later. What I learnt at that moment was that it is better to think about all this at leisure. If you want to be a good lover—and which man doesn't?—it is best not to think about fucking when you are fucking. At that time, you should distract yourself and think about other things. Think about the seventeen-times table or try and list the chief ministers of your state in order. Try and take your mind off the fact that you are doing what every man would rather be doing. If you think about fucking when you're fucking, you'll find you're not fucking any more.

In other words, you'll come.

That's what happened to me. Almost as soon as I entered her, I was done. I groaned and buried my face in her hair.

'Ho gaya?' She seemed matter-of-fact.

I nodded and rolled off and hid my face under my arm. And then she taught me a lesson.

'Hey, I'm not done here,' she said. She grabbed the arm and pulled it off my forehead. 'Get on with it.'

I did, but it wasn't the same. When you're hot and wanting it, you don't notice anything, you just want it all. You want the softness of hair and the rhythm of muscle under skin. You feel like she is the most beautiful woman in the world, you feel like she is the most desirable of all possible lays. But when you've dropped your load and your cock is shrivelling in the condom and you're beginning to wonder if it's going to leak on the floor, you begin to notice that there are three hairs on one nipple and you wonder if it is because of age. As you run your fingers through her pubic hair, you look now for signs of ageing. You see the sag of the triceps and the folds of cellulite on the upper thigh. You should not be noticing. You should be rejoicing. Is this not the woman you dream about? Is this not the moment that you have been savouring as you walked from house to house, as you witnessed the titanic struggle of Tehmi with trigonometry? How can you be so choosy, so particular, when only a month ago you would have given a couple of teeth for this moment?

However, Prema Jha seemed to know what turned her on. She was good at leading me to the spot marked X and telling me how to do what I needed to in order to get her where she wanted to go. I added some variations of my own, sometimes startling her, sometimes displeasing her, but almost never disconcerting her in the way I had on the first day, that first time.

How long did we go on like this? I suppose I could tell by looking at my bank account. I had decided that the money I made from my cocksmanship would go towards myself and I opened a separate bank account so that I could put the money away there. As soon as I was done, I made a bank run and tucked it away, out of my reach. When the bank issued me a cheque book, I took it and ceremoniously hurled it into the Arabian Sea. I was not going to touch that money.

There was a time when French lessons sometimes happened twice a week, and the money kept coming. And then, quite by accident, I discovered a way to make a little more.

One day, my mother complained that she was not feeling well. When I asked, she went coy on me and said that she could not explain. By this, I took her to mean that it might be gynaecological and I asked the sisters to take charge. They did, but the news was not good. Mummy had a large tumour inside her. It was the size, the doctor said, of a coconut. It had to be removed immediately and, with it, her uterus too. I thought that this would not be too much of a problem for a woman her age. She had been through an early menopause and so her uterus was pretty much not a functioning part of her body. It would be like taking her appendix out.

But on the day that she was to go to the hospital, she was found sitting on the bed, in a flood of tears. The sisters thought she was in pain, but she was not. She was weeping and would not say why. I thought she was weeping for the loss of her womanhood. I tried to imagine myself as an eighty-year-old man whose cock and balls have not done anything for him for ten years. But still he might have some issues if someone threatened to cut them off.

I sat down next to Mummy and tried to explain hormone replacement therapy, but she was not listening to me. She was crying and making sounds like a child. I had a flashback to my father sitting with her on the bed and trying to explain something to her and failing. He had taken her in his arms and cuddled her and hummed to her as if she were a child, so that was what I did. Finally, she stopped sobbing and the sisters stopped bobbing in and out like helpless ducks and I discovered what the matter was.

Nothing was the matter. She knew that the operation was routine. She knew that the tumour was probably benign. But she was scared. She told me about so-and-so who had gone in for a tooth extraction and had bled to death. She told me about such-and-such who had had a bad case of appendicitis and had come through the operation okay and was about to go home when he had developed a slight fever and then spent three days in the ICU and then died of organ failure. She told me about someone who had never drunk or smoked but had had a stroke while taking a blood test.

'Hospitals are there to kill you,' she said.

And it came down to this. She would go to the hospital, but only if all three of her children were there and if all three of them were visible to her when she went into the operation theatre because this might be the last thing she would ever see in her life.

I agreed.

So I made a hurried call to Prema Jha. Only, she did not pick up the phone, and I could not tell the old mausi who did what I wanted to say—that there would be no class that day. So I just did not go and instead went with my mother to the hospital.

I thought at first that I might be able to get away in time, but the admission process took hours. There was always another form to fill and another person to meet and another place to go and someone else to register with. But finally it was done and Mummy was wheeled into the operating theatre. My sisters began to cry noisily until I snapped at them and announced that I had to go and earn a living and they had better pull themselves together.

'When will you come back?' the older one asked.

'I don't know,' I said. 'Usual time.'

But, instead of going for tuitions, I just went home. It was lovely to be at home, alone. I made myself two sandwiches—one of bread and ghee and sugar and the other of bread and butter and the rasa of mango pickle—and a big cup of tea. Then I sat down in front of the television set and put in a video cassette of *Sholay*. I felt good and relaxed.

Then the phone rang. I picked it up and heard: 'Teri baahon mein hai jaanam, meri jism-o-jaan pighalte.' I hung up and started the film again. The phone rang after about five minutes and there it was again. Another Hindi film song playing: 'Tum bin jaaoon kahaan?' I began to wonder what was happening. The third time, I listened to a verse of the song and then said, 'Hullo?'

It was Prema.

'Why didn't you come today?'

I didn't know what to say. I thought I could tell her the truth, that my mother was in the hospital. But I was silent. Perhaps because the next question would be: 'So what are you doing at home?'

'I had some work,' I said.

'Oh,' she said. 'I'm sorry to hear that.'

Her voice was cold. I grew angry.

'Yes, I have to earn a living,' I said. 'I have a mother in the hospital and two sisters to marry off. I have a home loan to pay. Are you sorry to hear that as well?'

I banged the phone down.

I felt good. I felt bad. I had told the truth. I had lied. I had showed the rich bitch her place in the world. I had pushed away the only woman I knew who would give me sex for free. I could barely concentrate on the movie.

And then the sisters came home and began shouting about who had left the butter out of the fridge, and why had I left the spoon in the pickle, didn't I know it would get black?

That was when I knew that I had to get out of there. I had to find another home. I had to find another way to live.

The next morning, I was supposed to teach Pralay. To my surprise, Prema was also awake. Her eyes were swollen. If I had known then what I know about women now, I would have known that she had managed this somehow. But I was young and I was guilty. So I felt sorry for her.

'Sir, my math tests ka results,' said Pralay. I looked at them cursorily. Normally, this would be a time of some tension. Good marks mean you get to continue. Bad marks may even mean dismissal, although most parents will listen to some nonsense about their son having what it takes and just not paying attention, etc., etc. Pralay seemed to have done well. Sixty per cent was okay. In normal circumstances, I would have sighed and read him a little lecture over the missing forty per cent. Instead, I gave him a dazzling smile and said that he had done very well and watched with alarm as he responded with visible enthusiasm.

This was a turning point for Pralay, and I discovered it only by accident. You don't have to wait for ninety per cent to compliment the kid. You can do it when they've shown some improvement, and this gets them hooked. They want your approval—and they will work for it.

Idiots.

But it is idiocy that makes us all manageable. Prema's idiocy made her manageable too, for now she produced a watery smile and a Rolex watch.

'This is for you, sir,' she said. 'From all of us.'

'And I get nothing?' Pralay said.

For a moment, I looked at the watch and I thought to myself: 'Now you are a gigolo. This is exactly the kind of gift a rich woman gives to a gigolo.' And then I looked at the watch again and thought: 'That's only a word. I don't have to call myself anything I don't want to call myself.'

But my middle-class mind was still active and so, before I could stop myself, I was saying, 'I don't need anything for doing my duty.'

For a moment, venom flashed in Prema's eyes and she looked like she was going to take me seriously. Then Pralay saved the day.

'I need a watch, Mama,' he began to whine. 'And it's not fair. I did the work. I got the marks. And sir gets the watch. I don't see why I...'

So I got to take the watch. The whole family insisted, except for Mausi, who was looking on with clear eyes.

When I was leaving, she said, 'Sir, where you are going?'

I said I was going to the USIS to study. It was the truth.

'Sir, I am going that side only. I will give you drop.'

This seemed a little puzzling because Mausi did not appear to care much for me. I had thought this was a caste thing—that I, a Kayastha, was eating at her Brahminical table—but now she didn't seem to mind dropping me in her car?

'That flat?' she said, pointing across the corridor as we left the flat. 'Police are coming there.'

'Oh?'

'You know why?'

'No.'

'Because one gold bangle is going missing. There was one servant they had. He is a nice boy. A young boy. Big-made. Whatever work, he will put his hand. Not saying, no, for this I am not here, for that I am not here. He is just doing and helping.'

'Good. Such people are rare.'

'Haan, but that is first-first. Later, he is changing. He is becoming...how you say?' She frowned and pulled down the sides of her mouth.

The lift arrived.

'Surly?'

'Haan. Perfect.' She pronounced it to rhyme with 'defect'. 'He is becoming surly. This word I must learn because it is happening a lot to our servants.'

We got into the lift and went down five floors.

'You see, it is the way of the world,' she said. 'Servants are servants. This is how it is. How can we change the world?'

Bitch. But I felt that there was no way to argue with her. So I simply said, 'One cannot.'

'It is good for all of us to remember that,' she said. She stopped at the entrance to the building, where the names of the owners were inscribed on wooden plates in a variety of paints and fonts that could probably tell you something about the owners. 'P. Jha', it said in plain Roman. 'This house is in my name.'

'Really?'

'Haan. P here is for Panna, not Premlata.'

'Premlata?'

'She,' she said and jerked a thumb over her shoulder. 'Premlata, she was. After Baba, she began calling herself Prema.'

'After Pralay?'

'No, after Praveen.'

Praveen, I assumed, was the dead husband.

'Here,' she said, pointing to the ground beneath her feet. 'They found him here.'

'Who?'

'You don't know? Praveen. They found him here. When he fell.'

'Fell?'

'Five years ago. He fell. It was the first time the police came to the building. For us. For the Jhas.'

I tried to arrange my face to look sympathetic, but I was actually quite shocked. These things didn't happen in such buildings, did they?

'I told first only. I told Badi Bi,' continued Mausi.

'Who is Badi Bi?'

'She lives in that house. She owns it. I said, "If the boy is from the hills, he will be fair and he will be tall. Your son is here, there, here, there. But your bahu is here all the time." But she said, "I am here to see." Haan, we are there to see, but we are not there twenty-four hours. Some time for God. Some time to sleep. Some time to go and see sick friend. That is when it happens. I told her.'

I had thought she had been talking about the neighbours. Now I wondered.

'Then Badi Bi saw. It was getting bad. He would not give tea. He would put down tea like this, like you're giving a gali ka kutta some roti. He asked for one television set. When they did not give, he would put on television himself. And sit. In front. Arre, some servants in this building forty years, like that. They won't sit. He was sitting. Haq se. And the bahu was there.'

I sighed. I had no idea where this was going.

'Then it happened.'

'What?' I asked.

'Badi Bi lost her bangle. A big gold bangle. She called the police. They came and they searched the boy's boriya-bistar and they found the bangle in the middle of it. Just like that. How much he was crying, I did not do, I did not do. How much he was weeping when they took him away. I am told they beat him and beat him until he confessed.'

I felt a chill of horror down my spine.

'You see, you can say this is gone, you can say that is finished. You can say things are not like they used to be. But one thing is left. Police knows whose word to take. Badi Bi's word? Or the word of some boy from the village?'

She was warning me. The silly bitch was warning me. I lashed back.

'Whose word did they take? When they came for Praveen?'

I saw hatred in her eyes, clear as the full moon on Shivratri. She was declaring war on me.

'They took her word. They took my word. We said: "He went to hang up some lights and he slipped." That is what we said. But I know and she knows.'

What was she saying? That Praveen had been pushed? That he jumped? It was all getting too complicated for me. I got out of the car and then leant down to look in at the window of the ancient Ambassador.

'Thank you for your advice. Should I return this watch or will you go to the police?'

She smiled.

'That is your inaam. Pralay did better in mathematics. You may keep it.'

'And I'll even tell him to let you give him bath,' I said and I saw her face whiten and go taut. It was unfair and unkind, but the bitch was cutting me off.

I walked down to the arcade and asked about the prices of Rolex watches. It was incredible how different the price ranges were when you wanted to buy and when you wanted to sell. I asked after the older watches and found that I might get a better price were I to keep it for a while. I gave up the idea of selling it immediately and converting it into cash. There's something about cash that I like. It is what you want it to be. A watch, on the other hand, on whichever hand, is a watch. But I suppose it was better than burfi.

Because that was all I had been getting when the kids did better.

Burfi.

Often it was good burfi, but burfi nonetheless. So I began to show my Rolex to other parents when I thought that their tykes were doing well. I managed to score a nice pen, a silver card case and a rather lovely tie-pin simply by playing on the idea that it was the done thing to give the teacher something nice and non-edible, something to remember the child by when it was all over. These, I quickly turned into cash, and the cash into bits of gold. No stones, no beads, no shares. I like gold and I would buy it as soon as I could afford it and stick it in a safety deposit locker I had got for myself. The key? It was wrapped into a pair of socks.

The next time I went to meet Prema, I went up only when I saw the Ambassador trundle away with its burden of old women. Prema seemed to be eager for sex; she barely let me speak before she had me on the floor. I took her cue and gave it to her as she wanted it. My teeth were buried in the curve of her shoulder, my hips pumping frantically as she lashed her head from right to left. It was all over in a few minutes. When I reached between her thighs, she pushed my hands away. Obviously, she had managed to come.

'What did she say?' she asked.

I told her.

She stared at me.

'How did she know?'

'I told her,' I said sarcastically. 'How do I know? She has eyes in the back of her head. She has a spy in the building.'

'Hari Om!' she said.

'Hari Om!' I echoed.

'No, no, not like that. I mean, the building watchman. He is her pet dog.'

I sighed. 'Maybe it would be best to end this.'

'No, no, she cannot win. Let me think.'

I shrugged and got up and put on my clothes.

'Have a bath before you go.'

'No,' I said. 'I'm in a hurry.'

I don't know why I said it, nor do I know why I walked down the stairs when I left the building. Outside, I saw the Ambassador. I leant in and smiled at the driver.

'Kya hua?'

'Badi Mem ko chakkar aa gaya. Waapis aayi.'

She had thought to catch us red-handed. Someone up there was obviously looking after my interests. It was time to cut and run.

I gave Prema and Pralay one month's notice. Pralay didn't even notice. I had barely taught him a few months and there was no emotional bond between us. Prema was too sensible to want to jeopardize her position. She thought of various ways in which we could make it work. We could meet out of Bombay. Yes, we could, but that would mean going out of Bombay and I could not do that too often.

'I can give you what you will lose on the tuitions,' she said.

It wasn't quite that simple. A tutor who is irregular is no tutor at all. He loses reputation, he loses students and, eventually, he loses everything. I know. I've inherited a lot of these students. 'Sir, bas one thing,' one of the parents will say to me. 'Aap regularly aaya karo. That is all Munna needs. Regular.' I agree. It is almost always the answer. If you want to get better at something, do it regularly.

I suggested an easier way. She could hire me a small flat of my own. I could live there and she could visit whenever she wanted. She thought about that and then turned it down. She didn't have that kind of money. I looked at her.

She was living in a three-or-four-bedroom apartment that faced the sea. She could give me a Rolex watch when her son improved his maths score or I didn't turn up to service her. And she couldn't set me up in a love nest?

'It's not easy,' she said. 'I have to account for everything. The trust asks questions.'

Apparently, Praveen's death had raised many questions in the biradari. They had decided that his money would go into a trust. She got an allowance.

'If I handle it well, I can live well,' she said. 'But I can't afford anything like this.'

And so that was that.

I steadied myself with a long walk by the sea. I was not in love with Prema. I had enjoyed having sex with her. I had gained some money and a good watch. But I did not want to lose sight of my own objective. I wanted to earn enough money to buy my own house, to go back to my dream of becoming a lawyer. I would move on.

Nothing happened for a year or more. At least, nothing happened that would be of interest to relate here. I bought myself a second-hand motorbike, after much thought. I had resisted for a long time because I did not want to spend any money. Then I realized, after some calculations including the price of fuel, that it would mean savings for me. I could pack the students in closer instead of leaving fifteen-minute gaps for travel. I could sleep at least half an hour longer every day or spend more time in the gym, so there were even health benefits. My mother said it would be risky, but I knew that I was sensible and I would not go about riding like a madman. I want to live. The only downside was that my face got very dirty and so did my clothes—the dust blows and the wind forces it into the clothes—but the sisters were there to look after this. Besides, now I had some measure of freedom. I could travel anywhere in the city without thinking about how much time it would take.

The motorbike was also how I met Aparna.

She was standing at the bus stop at Nepean Sea Road, and she did not look like any of the other women who were standing there. For one thing, they were all in jeans and T-shirts and she was in a salwar kameez. It was not a khadi-type thing, but it was cotton. She didn't look like a rich South Bombay bitch. She stood out because she was a bit dark, but she didn't care—you could tell by how she held her body and how she stood. She knew she was beautiful.

I noticed that she got into a bus that was headed to Nana Chowk and I guessed that she was a Wilson College student. I didn't even think all this consciously, you understand, it was just going on inside my head. Haan, there she is, that indigo-blue-kurta girl again, only today it's black-and-red. And that bus, where will she be going? Okay, so...

One day, quite by chance, our eyes met. The next day, I sought out her eyes, but then I caught her glance and looked away. The next day, I smiled. Fourth-fifth day, she wasn't there. The day after, she was. I raised a hand and, before she could stop herself, she raised a hand too. And a couple of weeks after I had first noticed her, I stopped and said, 'Lift?'

One thing that always holds good in India: you cannot do anything on the quiet. The whole world stops to look at you. You would have thought that Amitabh Bachchan had come to pick up Hema Malini, the way everyone turned and looked.

'No, thank you,' she said.

'Come on,' I said. 'What can happen to you on a bike?'

She smiled and shook her head and didn't look at me. Great, I thought, and looked at the books she was holding against her chest. This is how all Indian girls stand: with their books in front of their breasts, so that roadside Romeos and cheapsters like me cannot get a good look or get a good feel.

The next day, I smiled, and she smiled back. But it was a yes-I-acknowledge-you-exist-but-don't-imagine-I-am-going-to-take-it-any-further smile. I didn't like that smile. So I just dipped my chin on the next couple of occasions that I passed.

To tell you the truth, I was rather busy elsewhere. After a few weeks, my luck seemed to be about to turn. I was teaching the sons of the owner of someone who made megabucks in a jink-mandi. I am joking, of course. This man was a metal dealer and he had made his money in zinc. He was now all set to take it global and he wanted his wife to be the kind of hostess who could speak English

Or so she said.

Her husband seemed to have very few opinions. He was a large man, not really obese, but one day his lungi fell open and his hairy thighs were visible. They were enormous, spreading at least a foot-and-a-half across. I felt a little sick looking at all that flesh and I promised myself that I would never let myself get that way. But already I could feel my muscle tone being compromised by the bike. I was riding it everywhere, as my friends had warned me I would. I fired it up to go to the market, which was about a hundred metres away from the house, for instance.

Mrs Jinks—as I will call her—was, in sharp contrast to her husband, a luscious lady. Everything about her was choice. She was in her early thirties and, though she wore only saris and kept her head covered, there was something about the way she moved that suggested something much more exciting. She was, I thought sometimes, like a river that is about to flood. Finally, she had hazel eyes. I find these unbelievably exciting. I don't know why. I know people say that people with light eyes are untrustworthy, but I don't believe it. Anyway, I didn't care. I was not looking for a life partner in her.

'When shall we study?' I asked and was immediately depressed when she asked if we could conduct the class directly after I had finished with Aniruddh. That meant she had no designs on my person. She was asking for a class in the middle of the evening, when the entire family would be present.

'Sorry,' I said. 'I won't be able to. That time is full up. How about eleven in the morning?'

'Tell him,' she said, and a certain feline satisfaction crossed her lips.

Mr Jinks looked bored. 'This means you will be coming two-two times?'

I agreed that I would.

'Arre, car bhej diya karo sir ke liye.'

I thought this uncommonly kind of him, but I saw the feline satisfaction evaporate. I began to suspect that these were rather deep waters. I had the feeling that I might get caught in a Roman Polanski script, where husband and wife do battle and some helpless third person gets caught in the middle.

But the helpless third person, I have thought, is always a bit silly. S/he can always walk away, and never does. I resolved that I would just walk away if things got too complicated.

I turned down the car politely.

'Arre,' said Mr Jinks, 'why?

I thought quickly. 'Sir, if the car is late, I am late. But if I am coming on my own, then I can always be on time.'

He looked unconvinced.

'Besides, your driver would have to come to a different place each time.'

'Haan, you go to different-different places,' he said, making me sound like someone slightly cheap.

But that wasn't him, I realized. It was me.

'Haan,' I said. 'Aaj kal, Saraswati gali-gali phirti hai.'

He looked abashed.

On the way out, I stopped to chat with the doorman. 'Jinks Saahab ka driver kaun hai?'

He looked at me, a slight expression of mistrust crossing his face. I offered him a pack of cigarettes. He took one and tucked it behind his ear. I had not seen anyone do that outside of the movies.

'Woh,' he said. 'Hero.'

I did a double-take. 'Woh?'

The man chuckled.

'Wohi,' he said. 'Ulti Ganga behti hai, bhaiya!'

He had pointed out a young man who looked like he was a film star. He had the jaw for it, certainly, and the carefully sculpted body. Nothing I could have done in the gym could have produced that effect. It was steroids and supplements, plus the genetic talent to keep it going. He was in spotless white, but his trousers were not the same material as his shirt, as befits those who wear uniforms for a living. He was wearing beige corduroy pants that seemed to have been stitched onto him, ridge by ridge.

'Naam kya hai?'

'Uska?' I thought of a snappy retort in the fashion of *MAD* magazine but decided against it. 'Armaan,' said the old man. He gave the word a slightly lewd tone. Was this the man I was replacing? Would he suddenly find a bangle in his glove compartment?

I felt a shudder run down my spine and then I thought of the swollen river, of my chances of taking a dip, and I stiffened my resolve. (I had stopped carrying a bag around after Panna Mausi's warning; it was irrational, I knew, because if someone is out to get you they're going to get you, but I was taking no chances.)

And so Aparna faded a little from my consciousness.

When you think there's the promise of sex, other things fade. Like love. Not that I was in love with Aparna—at that time, I did not even know her name, and I wasn't even sure that I wanted to know it. But I could tell from her clothes, from her bearing, from the way she held those books, that she was not going to fall into my lap and start undoing my zip. She would want a courtship and promises and dinner dates and all the rest of that. I was not averse to this. I can see why a woman might want such things and why a man might want to provide them for her, but I did not feel any pressing need to go down that road. 'Nalli saaf to sab kuchh maaf,' as my school buddies would have said.

Then one day, as I was riding down the road, I saw her wave at me. I waved back before I realized that hers was not a 'Hi' wave. It was a frantic wave. It was a wave that said: 'Stop, right now!' I could have ignored her and, truth be told, I was tempted to do so. After all, she had turned me down. And I could kind of guess that she wanted to go to college, while I was riding in the opposite direction. But I did slow down almost before I had made up my mind and then it was too late because she was beginning to run

towards me and again her body language spoke of panic.
To start again now, to ride off down Nepean Sea Road,
would have been tantamount to slamming the door in her
face. So I stopped, and she came running up to me.

'I have an examination in fifteen minutes,' she said. 'And
I missed my bus.'

'Get on,' I said.

She got on and immediately I could smell her fragrance.
It was nothing that came out of a bottle. Instead, it was all
earth and mud and richness. It was shikakai and herbs. It
was spicy and rich and completely feminine because there
was a trace of sweat in it, the sweat of her panic. She was
also, I was glad to see, no slippery side-saddle squatter.
Instead, she threw her leg over the machine, and the next
thing I felt were her arms looping around my waist and
the pert thrust of her breasts against my back. I started the
machine and we were off, south down Nepean Sea Road.

'Wrong way,' she shouted in my ear.

'Wrong way for the bus. Right way for you,' I shouted
back. 'I'll get you to college in time.'

'This is not the way,' she shouted again as I wove between
two cars and shot up the flyover near Priyadarshini Park.

'It is the way,' I shouted. 'Trust me'

We roared up Malabar Hill, and I ducked in and out of
a school of Japanese tourists looking at an old Jain temple
and then broke the signal at Walkeshwar and hurtled down
the road past Birla School. Several schoolgirls raised a cheer.
Aparna unlooped an arm to throw them a wave and a white

smile that flashed in my rear-view mirror. Then she shook her head into the wind and turned her face up to the sun.

I broke another two signals at Chowpatty, and we roared to a halt in front of Wilson College.

'Thanks,' she said.

'You owe me,' I said, allowing a flash of naughtiness in my smile.

'I always pay my debts,' she said. Then she turned and ran.

And I rode off again, happy in an odd way, in a way that even a swollen river could not manage.

The river was running thick and fast when I got to the home of the Jinkses. The house was empty, which seemed a little odd, but Mrs Jinks was also subdued, which seemed as well. I suggested we use the children's bedroom where I taught the young Jinkses, but she pointed wordlessly to the dining table in the hall. This was a bit depressing. Was I going to have to teach English? Oh, well. If so, so.

I suggested we start with 'I am, you are, he is, she is…' I had learnt what little French I knew through conjugations and thought it seemed a good enough way to begin since few people who don't speak English fluently ever get their tenses right.

She limped along with me willingly. 'I em, you aarr, he ij, she ij,' she said and kept casting sideways glances at me, as if she were expecting me to make some move. Since we were sitting side by side, I moved my elbow so it touched hers. Almost immediately, she withdrew her arm. And still those glances, increasingly coy. If ever there were mixed signals, hamin ast, hamin ast, hamin ast. And yet, the idea of the paradise she was promising drove me on. Having had my arm repulsed, I decided to use my knee and slowly slid it against hers. Once again, her knee moved away. But the glances were now almost frantic, her colour high and her breathing fast.

I gave up. I thought she might be afraid, so I brought it all down a notch. I began to take on, almost without knowing it, the demeanour I had with her children. I was stern and severe and clicked my tongue irritably when she made mistakes.

And then her elbow slipped and began to rub against mine.

I grew brusque and began to make sounds as if she were a retard whose dimwittedness I could not believe.

And her knee came up to mine.

Then the hour was up, so I decided to punish her and snarled: 'You are completely stupid and I cannot teach you.'

'Sorry, sir,' she said. 'Very, very sorry.'

But she was crooning it and seemed ready to come.

'And if I am to come again, you cannot dress like this,' I said, pointing to her salwar kameez.

'How to dress then?' she asked in Hindi.

'This also I will have to teach you,' I said.

'Haan,' she said. 'Maybe you should teach me how to dress too.'

I suspected irony and found none.

'Next time,' I said.

And when she turned around, I gave her a smart slap on her rear. She gasped and stood still, so I tried again. But there were too many layers between my hand and her for this to be any fun for me, even if it was clear that she was enjoying it. I decided to leave it alone for the moment.

'Ja rahe ho?' she asked as I prepared to leave.

I grabbed her by the shoulders and pushed my face into hers. 'Why should I stay? Yahaan rakha kya hai?' I smashed my lips against hers and, for a moment, she simply waited me out. And then the river burst its banks. Her tongue surged into my mouth, her fingers dug into my back and she raised one leg and coiled it around the back of my thigh, pushing her crotch into mine. We were evenly matched in height, we were evenly matched in passion, but something told me that it would not be a good idea to take this straight to the bedroom now.

'Chudail,' I said as I detached my mouth from hers. 'Rundi,' I whispered as I ran my tongue from cheek to ear. 'Daayan,' I said as I nipped the earlobe from which a solitaire dangled. I was so close to her that I could see the blood running under her skin. 'And this is for punishing me,' I said, pulling away.

I left, although she was moaning for more.

The next time, she was as good as her word. She was wearing only a huge Turkish towelling robe, which I could see had come out of a Taj Mahal Hotel. It is incredible how cheap the rich can be. However much there is to be made in metal, they will try and get a little more for their money's worth, a towel here, a bathrobe there. I promised myself I would never do that kind of thing when I was rich.

She beckoned me into her bedroom.

'What I will wear?' she asked. She said wear to rhyme with here.

I thought I might correct her, but she had dropped her towel and was facing me, naked. She was reflected in the mirrors of her wardrobe, so I could see her reflected, every view I could want.

There is an Indian woman who is seen as cosmopolitan. Indeed, she is. Her hair ripples like silk and her walk promises the magic of a woman who is willing to look you in the eye while sucking on your big toe. But the rest of her body has withered into a reptile. She has lost weight and turned into a stick insect. This means she pleases no one but herself—and how often we are told that she dresses, she uses make up, she does whatever she does to her body, only for herself.

But here, in front of me, was the wish-fulfilment of any Indian man. Here was a woman willing to transform herself into the houri of his desires. Here was a woman in the fullness of her womanly splendour: her hair was that black silky river and her eyes were electric with desire, her lips were parted—but who cared about all that? I could not look above her breasts and beneath her hips. Here was delight.

'You do not have to dress,' I said. 'Today we will study parts of the body.'

She pretended to look coy and reluctant. This, you can imagine, must have been something of a feat since she was nude and had dropped her dressing gown voluntarily. But then, almost at the moment that I was going to give in, I realized that this was part of her game.

'You are not going to obey me?' I snarled, and she began to cower against the wardrobe. I pulled her into my arms and, for an instant, I was almost overwhelmed by the feminine pulchritude in my arms. But I caught hold of myself.

I was not here to enjoy myself, I told myself only half-mockingly. I was here to earn myself a house so I could enjoy it later. And how would I enjoy myself then? I had to shake away the thought of my father and my mother and the three of us, all living together, all of us locked into a nightmare of modern city life, where you send your children to the movies when you want to cop a feel of the wife to whom you are legally married.

I forced the thought out of my mind. If I were to pay attention to it, what might happen? All my life, I had seen myself as a certain person, and that certain person had a certain way of getting ahead. This involved getting married and having kids and having a house and having a career. As I bit into Rewa's neck, why did this seem like a plan that had belonged to someone else?

She was moaning by the time I reached down to pinch

a berry-pink nipple with my fingers. I pushed her down so that she was crouching in front of me. And then I turned her head and ground it into my crotch. She looked up at me and said, 'Nahin, woh main nahin kar sakti.'

I kicked her from me and pretended to walk away. She lay on the ground moaning but caught hold of my ankle.

'Acchha, baba,' she said. 'Jo tumko ho pasand, wohi karenge.'

I sat down on the edge of the bed and looked at myself in the mirror. Here I was, sitting on the bed of a room where each square foot cost more than my monthly wages. Here was the co-owner of this house, squatting nude between my feet. She reached for my belt, but I pushed her away.

'Start with my feet,' I said, and she looked confused. I translated, and she got it. She was a quick study and was licking my toes eagerly in a moment, spread out in front of me like a slave. I had never, in all my solitary morning excavations into the world of my fantasies, ever thought up something like this. My fantasies were drawn from Hindi films: Hema Malini tearing my shirt and jeans open as she slid, her feet torn by glass, down the front of my body; Sridevi rippling her body against mine and discovering the thorns that would stab her...that kind of thing.

And I knew what I had to do.

'Stop it,' I said. 'Enough.'

And I got up and left.

Like that.

I don't know why, but it was the perfect thing to do.

When I went to teach the little Jinkses, another watch happened. I had begun to understand how to function.

I wore the watch to have coffee with Aparna. I took her to the Sea Lounge; it seemed like the thing to do. She had protested in the way women do. 'Oh, it's too expensive,' she had said when I called her at her friend's house. (I wasn't allowed to call her at home, she hadn't even given me her number, what if her family found out about me?) At the same time, she had also managed to convey her excitement about being taken to a posh joint, her realization that she had to matter to me for me to take her there.

Did she matter then? I don't think so. I took her there because I could. It felt good to be able to waste money.

'You have a great watch,' Aparna said, sitting at a window-side table, looking out to the sea. 'It's an antique, I think.'

'How do you know?'

'My father has a collection of watches,' she said. 'I've seen one like that. It costs a lot.'

I looked at the watch again and with more respect.

The next time I went to the Jinkses, I wore the watch. Rewa was again nude, but I said carelessly, dismissively, 'Put on some clothes.'

'Why?'

'Because I say so, bitch,' I said and slapped her on the buttocks.

She flushed and went off to change. I followed her.

'No,' she protested. 'You don't look.'

I leant down casually and bit her nipple. Hard.

'No?' I asked.

'No,' she said again, this time flinging a challenge at me.

I grabbed her and dragged her to the bed. I sat down on it and pulled her across my knees. And then I spanked her. She gasped and began to wriggle. Her thighs began to twist against each other, like copulating snakes. A few more strokes, and she had had an orgasm. How do I know? It was unmistakable, the way her body bucked and rocked, as if every bone inside it were possessed of a desire to move in the direction opposite to the bone next to it.

She rolled off my knee.

'Padhaai karein?' I asked.

She looked startled and then she smiled. She went to the wardrobe, but I said, 'Nahin, come like that only.' She looked even more startled, but walked nude, elegant, in control, to the dining room and to the table.

'There is only one way to learn a language,' I said. 'You must talk it.'

She cocked her head and smiled at me. She was so stunning and that smile was so effective, I wondered why she would need to learn any language at all. She would be able to win friends, influence people and do whatever she wanted, if she could only keep smiling like that. Perhaps it helped that she was in the nude and that her breasts were sitting on the edge of the table, like two plump doves.

'Okay,' she said.

'So talk.'

'Do you like vaatch?'

'Did you like the watch?' I corrected.

'Did you like the vaatch?' she parroted.

'Yes, I liked the watch,' I said and stroked one of the doves.

'It is my father,' she said.

'It belonged to my father,' I said.

'Belong?'

I explained.

'You belong me,' she said.

How does anyone ever learn a language they haven't learnt as a child?

'No,' I said. 'You belong to me,'

'Wohi toh.'

'Stand up,' I said.

She did. The seat of the chair was wet. Her essence.

I ran a finger in it.

'Chhee,' she said.

'Clean it up,' I said.

She moved to get a cloth.

'No,' I said, a master again. 'With your tongue.'

As she crouched there, I undid my trousers and pulled out my cock. I got a condom on without tearing it—some feat, that—and bent over her. I thrust into her and she screamed, but more for effect than out of pain, I thought. I began to fuck her as a dog might fuck a bitch, hard and fast. She was so wet that I could barely keep my cock from slipping out of her. When I felt my orgasm roaring into my head, filling my body with its heat, I let my body drop onto hers. She bore me heroically.

Then the lesson was done and I left with a pair of cufflinks. I did not know if they belonged to her father. I didn't care. They seemed to be made of gold. Of course, they weren't. They were gold-plated and the stone in them was badly flawed. Net worth? Much less than the watch.

It was time to be cruel so that I could be kind to my bank account.

And so, for a week, I cut her off. I did not visit the house. I did not see the children.

Finally, on Sunday, a call came. One of my sisters took it and said, 'It's from the father of one of your pupils.'

This was rare. Education was part of what some jocular men would call the home minister's portfolio. In other words, when the children did well, they would claim the credit. When the children did badly, it was the mother's negligence. As for all the paraphernalia involved in education, in the selection and paying of tutors, all that was also part of what wives did.

Thank heavens for that.

It made my job a little easier.

'Sir, aap to aate nahin hai?' said Mr Jinks.

I explained that I had not been well.

'Sir, you tell to me the real problem. Armaan has seen you in the area, day-night, day-night. Means you are well to teach other's children. Why not mine?'

Armaan again.

'Well,' I said. 'I will talk to you businessman to businessman. I have been offered more money...'

'Arre, since when we are kanjoos? Take the money you want, tell what it is, we will give. Now, please, you start tomorrow.'

I did indeed start again the next day with the little Jinkses. I gave one of them the cufflinks and told him to give them to his mother.

'Kiska hai?' he asked, slightly suspicious.

'Speak English or you get a kattoos,' I said. I find that boys respond well to the threat of violence. It makes them feel like men. I would not administer the knuckles-to-forehead, but just the threat of it keeps them in line. Girls are easier; sarcasm is cheap and effective.

'Like kattoos is English, na?' he replied. I rather liked him, the little Jinks. He had his mother's skin and eyes. More than that, he had charm—and this came out of not being loved enough. This made him want to please you and wanting to please you meant he tried a little harder.

'Who is this?'

'Whose are these?' I corrected him.

'Wohi toh.'

I gave up the unequal struggle.

'You'll get punished. They are your mother's. She lent them to me.'

He opened the box.

'It is nice.'

'I know.' I said. But I did not add: 'They are valueless.

And I prefer old watches with value to cufflinks that look nice but are gold-plated with flawed stones and have no brand name attached.' He might have thought the less of me.

'They were my father,' she said the next day, her eyes a bit red. I wondered if she had been weeping for me or if she had organized a little redness of eye in order to persuade me that she had been weeping. We had finally got around to body parts and I had derived much pleasure out of making her say cunt again and again.

Then we had moved on to my body and, finally, I had allowed her to touch me and to grope my cock. But only from behind cloth. When she had tried to undo my trousers, she had earned my ire and got herself another spanking. This had ended our sex session and I was now sipping coffee and she was dressed in a T-shirt and jeans.

'I do not want your father's whole wardrobe,' I said.

'Okay,' she said. 'Take this.'

And she gave me a coupon for five thousand rupees for clothes. I shrugged. I didn't need it, but the girls could do with some clothes. But then I had a flash. I went to the shop and cornered the young manager.

'How much cash will you give me for this?'

He looked at it and shrugged.

'Nothing,' he said.

I realized that there was nothing in it for him, so I waited until someone came up to the counter with a sizeable purchase. Her bill was seven thousand, and she willingly gave me four thousand in cash when I spun her a story about needing it for my mother's ill health.

I walked out of the store with four thousand rupees but with the feeling that this needed to be made simpler. I needed to be able to convert stuff into cash. Or I had to work out a way to make the women pay.

The idea itself was simple. I was offering a service. They were actually hiring me for it. They should pay. But this intersection of commerce and sex made them uneasy. Presumably, they wanted to believe that I wanted them for themselves, maybe even for their minds. They wanted love.

I was not offering love. I was offering sex.

Would I earn more if I pretended that I was in love with them?

This may have been the first time—outside that fancy shop, on my way to the bank, with four thousand rupees in my pocket—that I began to think of this as a career. Up until then, it had simply been a bonus. I was being paid and I was getting my tubes cleared and I was picking up in confidence. I don't think I would have ever thought of speaking to Aparna or taking her to the Taj if it were not for the fact that I had satisfied two mature and upper-class women. On the debit side, I had been scared away from one. By an old woman.

I tried not to think about that. And I tried very hard to conjure up the kind of person who would please Rewa.

You may think it is easy to have a slave, but it actually takes a lot of work. They want you to snarl at them all the time, and if you take some time off they try to do things to irritate you. This is particularly stupid because most of these things are not exciting at all. For instance, I said to Rewa that she should spend the next ten minutes as my footstool, crouched on the floor. I did not particularly want this; what I did want was how wet and ready she would be afterwards. A little humiliation went much further than the endless quantities of foreplay that every other article about sex suggested.

It sometimes disturbed me that she would be weeping as I entered her. It was as if she were sending out two messages at the same time: the first was that she hated me and all that we were doing; the second was that she was enjoying it immensely. I didn't know what to make of it—so I made nothing of it, and continued to enjoy her body for some months.

Meanwhile, Aparna thought I was a real gentleman.

'Thank you,' I said. 'And why is that?'

It was a Sunday evening in April. April is indeed the cruellest month on the pocket of the tutor. There's a small burst of activity at the beginning of the month as the year comes to an end and everyone wants extra time. Then the exams are over and, as we say in my part of the world, 'The fever breaks, the doctor dies.' The family calms down. The child is set free. The holiday, once a distant plan, is now reality. There is shopping to be done and promised treats to be redeemed. Who wants to see a tutor then? Only those who are preparing for the tenth standard, but even these eager beavers want Sundays off.

This means much less money, but it also means more free time. In another era, I would have spent this time reading Fyzee on Muslim law or Salmond on torts, but my dream of practising seemed to be fading fast. When I got angry with a kid for not doing his homework or for not living up to his potential, I did not think: 'What am I doing wasting my time with this boy when I could be working under Pitlawala and Surajmukhi?' Now my anger expressed itself as: 'What am I doing wasting my time with this boy who may do badly and ruin my reputation as someone who can bring home a ninety per cent or above?' It was a shift in who I was. Part of this shift was also due to Aparna.

'It's teaching,' she said earnestly when I disparaged what I did. 'Why do we despise tutors so much and respect teachers so highly?'

I shrugged. I didn't really care. 'Maybe it's because teachers are paid so badly that we try and make up for it by offering them respect?' I suggested.

'And tutors are paid so well that we see them as scum? I don't know. I don't think tutors are even paid that well… are they?'

This was dangerous territory. Why was she asking?

'Why?' I asked lightly. 'Are you afraid I'll stick you with the bill?'

We were sitting on the top floor of Café Naaz, one of the nicest ideas that the city has had. It is perched on Malabar Hill and, in the evening, you can watch as the sun dunks itself in the sea and the lights begin to come on. If you don't remember what it looks like, try *Qurbani* with Feroze Khan and Zeenat Aman. The fight sequence in which Vinod Khanna rescues Zeenat Aman takes place at Naaz.

'No, I was just thinking of the maid who works for us. She has two children and she was telling me that she pays two hundred rupees for their tuition.'

'Where does she live?'

'I don't know. Kandivali, I think.'

'Oh, in the suburbs things are different.'

'Yes, but you know, she pays two hundred rupees and some woman teaches them...'

'Does she come and teach them, or do they go to her?'

'That all I don't know. Why?'

'Makes a difference. If she comes home, then she's their tutor. If they go to her house, they're her tuition pupils.'

'Good grief, what does that mean?'

'It's not just a semantic difference; it's an economic difference. If I am your tutor, you get my services for that hour. It means I only get what you pay me for that hour. If you are my tuition pupil, I charge you a certain amount, but I may also charge others the same amount for the same time.'

'Chhee!'

'Okay. What are their names?'

'Whose names?'

'The names of your maid's kids?'

'I think…no, I've forgotten. Something generic. No wait, the names rhyme. Yeah, that's it. Ajay and Vijay maybe, or Rajan and Sajan?'

'Okay. Let's call them Ajay and Vijay. And let's call their teacher Mrs Pai. If Mrs Pai comes to Ajay and Vijay's house, she is going to teach them alone. And she will get two hundred rupees at the end of the month. If Ajay and Vijay come to Mrs Pai's house, they may find Sujoy and Bijoy also there. Namita and Nirmita may also be there. Each of them will pay two hundred rupees.'

'But that's exactly like a tutorial class?'

'Not really. Classes can have fifty kids in a single room sometimes. Here the maximum will be six or seven.'

'Why? What's to stop her from putting in fifty?'

'Space. Mrs Pai probably lives in the same slum as all her students. She probably has her own kids and her in-laws all living in the same space. How will she put bums on seats if she doesn't have seats?'

'Gosh, it's a business.'

'See? Now you're already seeing Mrs Pai as some kind of parasite of the poor. She is probably just making a living too, trying her best to get out of the slum or chawl or whatever it is. That's why tutors don't get any respect.'

'You seem to have thought all this out,' Aparna said.

Had I? I suppose I had. You get a lot of time to think

while you're in the bus queue or on the bus; less when you're on a motorbike.

And that's when she told me she respected me.

'Because you're willing to wait,' she said. 'You're not trying to get me into bed.'

There seemed to be a faint hint of puzzlement in her voice. Good. Puzzled women are going to spend more time thinking about you. Puzzled women are also a little off-balance.

I smiled. 'You don't know how much it costs.'

She pretended not to understand.

'There's nothing I'd like more than to leap over the table and show you that I'm not a gentleman,' I said. 'But don't worry…'—she wasn't looking worried, though, only mildly intrigued—'I'm not going to try that, much as I'd like to.'

'There is a via media,' she said, and we walked down Marine Drive in the late evening and then we sat by the sea and listened to the waves murmuring against the sand and we kissed and it was something special.

How was it special? I don't know. It felt like I had been eating hotel food for so long that I had forgotten what home food tasted like and someone had cooked me a meal. It felt like love.

My heart swelled up and I noticed clinically that my penis remained unaffected. I was enjoying this so much— the smell of her body, so fragrant and rich with spice; the touch of her hair, raw silk and midnight-black in the light of the stars; the feel of her against me; the suggestions of other textures under the slipperiness of silk, the possibility of roughness of hair, the tension of muscles. I was enjoying it more than I thought I could, but I was not aroused. I was a little annoyed at myself. I should be hot and hard. What if she reached down…?

The improbability of such a thing happening made me want to laugh and I wondered at how many emotions a person can feel all at once. No Indian middle-class girl was going to reach down and feel a man's cock—not during the first few kisses, at any rate. She had to be guided there, and when she got there she would do everything as if under pressure, only for love, because it's her duty, all of the above.

But the idea that she might touch me produced the first sparks and the first sparks are generally all it takes. I was hard in a few seconds and wondered whether I could risk pushing my hips against hers. Except, she was sitting next to me and only with a lot of manoeuvring would this be possible. And since I didn't want to lose the good impression I had created, I decided against it. I would content myself with her mouth and her face and not even reach for a breast.

Of course, as soon as the thought struck, the need began. I wanted to feel her breast and it was only with a great exercise of the will that I could stop myself.

Lesson learnt: stay in the moment. If you start thinking about something, even in a negative sort of way, the mind begins to respond inappropriately.

Eventually, a cop stopped the kissing party, with the usual questions about what we were doing there, how could we be doing such a thing since we looked like we came from good families, why we weren't getting married, whether we knew how much pain we were causing our parents. I kept a steady pressure on Aparna's hand because I had no intention of letting her get mouthy. After all, this was a Bombay cop, and Bombay cops only start moralizing when they smell money slipping out of their hands.

So I apologized profusely and grabbed both his hands and stuffed a hundred-rupee note into them. Aparna was scandalized.

'How could you do that?'

'Why? Did you want to spend the rest of the evening at the police station?'

'Of course not. But I don't see why…'

'Was it your money?'

'No,' she said, but I could sense that this was not the tack to take.

'Did I ask you for a contribution?'

'No.' She didn't say the word so much as let it slip from between her teeth.

I raised an eyebrow. 'So?'

'It's the principle of the thing.'

'Explain that to me,' I said.

'We were doing nothing wrong.'

'To which I added something wrong?'

'I didn't say that.'

'You meant it.'

'I did, okay, I did. But I don't think bribing a cop is right.'

'I don't think getting a woman into trouble with the cops is right either.'

'But how is he going to get me into trouble?'

'If a cop wants to get you into trouble, he can. It doesn't matter to him because he's only doing his job.'

'He's not.'

'Don't give me that why-aren't-they-running-after-real-criminals stuff. There's nothing in the law that says: "This is a real criminal and that's a false one." If you break the law, you're a criminal. And there's always a law about public morality or public decency.'

'I just don't want you doing that again.'

'I won't. And we won't kiss either.'

'That's ridiculous.'

'Can we make out at your place?'

'No. Are you nuts?'

'And we can't make out at my home either because my mother will throw us out. That means we have nowhere to go unless we rent a hotel room.'

'Oh gosh, that would be infra dig.'

I didn't know what that meant, but I guessed it meant something not nice. 'I am glad, however,' I said, 'that you did not issue a nolle prosequi.'

She looked startled. 'You studied law?'

'No,' I said. 'P. G. Wodehouse.'

She giggled and got onto the bike. This time, I could feel her breasts pushing against me. I had never felt them that way before, which told me something about how she sat, told me something about our kissing, told me something about where we were going.

I began to wonder whether I could get myself a room somewhere. We could have some privacy then. One part of me said, 'You can't get a room somewhere without causing yourself financial loss and slowing down the process of buying your own home.' Another part of me said, 'You know what buying a home costs in the city. You will be in your thirties by the time you're sitting in the bank and signing something. And what will be the use then? You will have to get married and settle down.' I knew which part this was. It was my dick talking.

So, when I had my evening bath, I masturbated so that I would stop thinking about another room in which I could teach children for part of the day and fuck women for another part of the day. Of course, it helped that my mother began to ask whether we had seven lakhs in the bank, as if she did not check the numbers almost every other day.

'Why do you need seven lakhs suddenly?'

'Suddenly?' she said. 'Suddenly, you're saying. As if you live in another world.'

If I go out to work, I come home and am received by Mother Number 1. This one is a pleasant person who wants to give me dinner and lay out nicely ironed pyjamas.

If I go out for any other reason, I am received at home by Mother Number 2. This one is a harridan who claims I do nothing, except for those things that make me happy. I once asked her about this and she went into hysterics and said I was calling her Number 2, so I just bear it. The only thing to do is to repeat the question and ignore the shit that gets thrown at you in between.

'Why do you need seven lakhs?' I asked again.

'I need. Yes, I will buy gold for myself. I will go to foreign. I will do this. I will eat in big-big restaurants.'

She had found the bill for the coffee Aparna and I had drunk. You would have thought I had sold one of my sisters into the sex trade. 'Four hundred rupees for two cups of coffee?' she had shrieked. I tried to convince her that a parent of one of my students had taken me out for coffee—which was true, only just not those two cups of coffee—but she was not convinced. 'So why do you have the bill? Surely he should have the bill! So much money wasted. On top, you are now telling lies.' That kind of thing.

I told myself now that I would not respond to her, I would not let her derail her own train of thought. This was difficult because I was beginning to feel the first spurts of rage against the backs of my eyes.

'Why do we need seven lakhs?'

'For Radhika.'

'A dowry?'

I looked beyond her form. Radhika and Anita were both present and correct.

'Dowry means what? You're talking like one journalist. Ek rishta aaya hai.'

I quelled the urge to say: 'And you're talking like a lyricist.'

'And?' I said instead.

'And means what?'

'So why do we need seven lakhs? Is that the dowry amount or is that the full-and-final figure?'

Radhika began to shift about uneasily. 'Bhaiya…'

Mummy turned to her like a cat defending its young. 'Shut up. Rani banke raaj karegi tu,' she said to Radhika. Then she turned to me again. Suddenly, she was all sugar and spice. 'You listen. This is a good offer. The boy is stable. And mature. He will look after her well.'

I knew what that meant. He was old. 'Widower? Divorced?'

Radhika burst into noisy tears.

'He is an innocent divorcee,' said my mother somewhat mystifyingly.

'Means?'

'Means? Everything I should tell? Nothing you will know?'

I thought about it. The term had come into being to describe women who had got married and then been abandoned but without ever having experienced the delights of the conjugal bed—or so their families tried to claim. This generally involved long, complicated stories about the health problems of the groom which had been concealed, but more often than not it was a simple sham. It meant: 'My daughter got married to a man from America, who then went back and filed divorce papers.' What they did not say was that the daughter had had sex with the man. Of course she had. Which man would not exercise his conjugal rights?

I sighed dramatically. 'I cannot manage this much,' I said. 'But if it means so much to you, I will get a loan.'

Radhika began to weep even more noisily. I should have guessed something was wrong then, but I was sick of all this. If the two had been working, I wouldn't have had to give up all my money—and borrow some—in order to pay for the wedding.

'But let the marriage be in May,' I said.

'Why May?'

'Because there are very few tuitions then. Otherwise, in all the running about, I will lose even more money.'

In the night, I heard something that shocked me to my core.

'What will become of us?' It was Anita.

'Means?' Now Radhika was speaking.

'How will it be? The sister of a tuition teacher?'

'Arre, who asks when there is money?'

'Yes,' said Anita. 'But see what they're asking. For an old man. Innocent-shinnocent, I don't care. For a man like that, no one has face to ask. Yet, they're showing face.'

'Don't worry about it. There's a way.'

I didn't hear the rest of it. All I could think was: tuition teacher, tuition teacher, tuition teacher. The bitches were happy to eat that money. Then there was no tuition teacher, tuition teacher. Then there was only this is needed, that is needed, bhaiya, that is also needed, please buy this for me. Not that I grudged them anything because they had been kept out of any thought or understanding of economy at my mother's insistence on keeping them out of harm's way. Not that I grudged anybody anything. But then, to bite the hand that feeds you by saying, 'tuition teacher', as if it were a profession without a pedigree...

The next day, when I came home, I found out what Radhika had meant by saying that there was a way. There was tension in the house when I entered. Mummy was sitting on the floor, the pallu of her sari pressed into her mouth.

'What happened?' I asked Anita.

'Radhika.'

I looked at my mother. She began to cry.

'She has run away,' she said between sobs. 'Ask her. She knows.'

I looked at Anita.

'What I know?' Anita was pretending. She knew.

'What is going on?' I asked. 'Where is Radhika?'

Now Anita began to cry as well.

'That boy...' Mummy burst into sobs again.

'Which boy?'

Anita ran off and locked herself in the bathroom.

'Muslim...' my mother moaned.

Muslim? Radhika had run away with a Muslim?

'I told you...' Mummy began.

'What did you tell me? I told you to send them to work and you said that they would spoil the name of the family. Now what good has come of that? Has she earned any money? No. Has she kept the name of the family? No. So how is this my fault now?'

Mummy started to weep and beat her breast. I couldn't take it, so I stood up and said, 'I'm going to the police.'

At which, my mother got hysterical. 'No police, no police. What will everyone say? How will I show my face to the world?'

I suddenly thought about Panna Mausi talking about the day the police came. 'Then what do you want me to do?'

'Go and find them and bring her back. Bring my daughter back.'

'Sure,' I said. 'Just like that.'

This only caused a fresh storm of tears. I went and knocked on the door of the bathroom.

'Who is this boy?'

'I don't know anything,' Anita shouted shrilly. It was clear from the tone of her voice that she knew a hell of a lot.

'Who is this boy?' I thundered, thumping on the door.

Anita began to cry loudly. I continued to thump, but then the doorbell rang. Mummy got up and began to totter to the door, presumably in the expectation that Radhika would walk in and all would be right again. I pushed her to the sofa and went to the door.

It was Sethi Mausi from next door. She was not a real relative, but when you have lived on top of each other for more than twenty years, some relationship tag has to be given. So, Sethi Mausi.

'Sab khairiyat?' Sethi Mausi was from Lucknow and had never let anyone forget that.

I shrugged and smiled and tried to close the door, but Sethi Mausi was not to be denied. She had already insinuated some of her body, slippery in a housecoat made of synthetic material, into the door. I could not close it without doing her—or the door—some damage. I yielded to the inevitable and let her come in.

'Kya hua, behen?' she asked and settled down near Mummy, with the air of a hungry but well-mannered vulture.

I said there was nothing the matter at the same time that my mother said that the family name had been ruined and our collective nose had been chopped off by my sister.

'Those boys are like that only,' said Sethi Mausi.

'Which boys are like what only?'

'M-type!' whispered Sethi Mausi. This was difficult because there were two M-types who ruled Sethi Mausi's view of the world of villains. One: the members of a parochial group; the other: members of a religious group. A perfect city would have neither M-type.

'Do you know anything about him?'

'Arre, what I'll know? Do I have time to die? How I am going to find out where and what and who? But everyone knows that he is the only educated member of his family. Otherwise, one brother is a loafer type—he can be seen sitting on a charpai near those wood shops. The other is a driver. Three daughters they have. God knows where they will put our Radhika.'

For someone who knew nothing, Sethi Mausi seemed to know almost everything about our in-laws.

Anita came out of the bathroom. And, in the way of these things, they began to compete about the information they had. It would seem that Radhika had met this boy when she had suffered a fall outside a temple. She slipped on a banana peel (Sethi Mausi), no, on a plastic bag filled with food (Anita), and Imraan had helped her to her feet. She had suffered a moch (Sethi Mausi), sprain (Anita), same thing (Mummy), and he had put her on his bike and taken her to a clinic and had sat with her while she was waiting for the doctor. He had told her that he was an engineer (Sethi Mausi), a computer engineer (Anita), same thing, please why didn't anyone ever tell me (Mummy). She had succumbed to his charms (Sethi Mausi), she had had jadu tona done on her in that clinic because she had come home with that black oil and those oils have herbs in them and dead lizards and God only knows what else (Mummy). Then he had met her the next day and the next and everyone had seen them at the shamshaan ghaat (Sethi Mausi)…

'Arre, marey merey dushman, why the shamshaan ghaat?'
Mummy, queen of the non sequitur, asked.

I did not explain that it was a long wall that stretched
for about five hundred metres and was faced only by the
sea. You could sit there and kiss there, and this was when
dupattas and pallus came in handy because they could be
used to create a little tent within which you could proceed
a little further than kissing.

And now the truth began to out. Mummy had known
about this all along.

'I showed you the sand,' said Anita. 'But you said she
was doing exercise.'

Since I paid for gym memberships for both my sisters, I
thought this a particularly silly excuse.

'So where does this boy live?'

I was told where and I sighed a little. It would be necessary
for me to go and see. It was not a desirable neighbourhood,
but it was not far away.

'What to do now?' said Sethi Mausi, with the delighted
air of someone who sees a situation as past redemption.

'Go now,' said my mother.

'Their marriage is simple. The girl has to say kabool and
the boy gets to jump. Finished. She is now Ayesha Begum.'

'Maybe she is not. Maybe not yet. You go and talk to
her,' Mummy said.

'They all become Ayesha Begum. Even that actress, what
was her name? You know, where I go to see Hindi films?'

'Hema Malini,' said Anita.

'Haan, she. She also became Ayesha Begum. I don't know why. It is not even such a good name.'

'Will she listen to me?' I asked. I thought it unlikely, but I went and got my socks and began pulling them on.

'Of course she will listen to you, you are her elder brother.' Mummy was protesting because she felt she had to. I knew there was no point to this. She knew this too. Then I looked at her and realized that she wanted to show that she had some control over her children. She wanted Sethi Mausi to see this too.

An imp made me ask: 'And you are her mother. Are you coming?'

'What will I do there?'

I wanted to say you will cry and weep and make such a fuss that she might even consider coming back.

Sethi Mausi was gleaming. She piped up: 'I feel sick at the smell of so much meat cooking. But, of course, if you need me I can come.' She said this with so much hope that you could tell she wanted me to ask.

I did not ask.

It was now ten-thirty and I wanted nothing more than to have a bath, eat dinner, catch up with the news and go to sleep. Sethi Mausi was probably right. This rescue act was doomed to failure. If Radhika and this boy had planned it well, the marriage would have happened in the early part of the day and the consummation in the evening, and then it would be a done deal. No going back on a broken hymen.

As I walked towards the area that was to be Radhika's new home, I felt the strange beginnings of something akin to relief. Because Radhika had taken herself out of my equation. She did not have to be provided for. A love marriage meant no horse-and-carriage, at least not from the girl's side. Now if only Anita could find love, if only some banana peel/plastic bag full of Udipi restaurant food would...

Of course, life was about to deal me a bouncer.

Mastani Manzil, I had been told, and it was quite apparent which building it was. There was a bunch of boys waiting outside it. I approached slowly, wondering if this was a good idea. Across the road, I saw a police jeep. Okay, if anything happened...

And then one of the figures in the group separated and began to walk towards me. It was as if he expected to be recognized. And then I saw who it was.

'Armaan?' I asked.

'Teacher Saahab,' he said.

'What are you doing here?' I asked, then felt silly.

'I live here,' he said. And then: 'Your sister is upstairs. She is married to him. Better you should go home now and tomorrow morning everyone can talk.'

I was slightly startled by his tone. 'How do you know where my sister is?'

'Because she has just become my bhabhi,' he said.

I stared at him for a moment and then the penny dropped.

The engineer had two brothers. Another figure detached itself. I presumed it to be the other brother, the loafer.

'Teacher Saahab,' said Armaan, indicating me with his chin.

The young man put out his hand. I took it by instinct and shook it. Cheers and whistles broke out from the group of boys behind. By this innocuous and instinctive act, I had signified my consent.

'Tomorrow morning,' I said. 'I will meet you tomorrow morning.'

As I turned to leave, I could see the cops revving up to leave too. It was over.

All I could think on the way home was: 'My brother-in-law is a driver.' And I realized guiltily that I had no business being angry with my sister for thinking of me as a humble tutor. If I did not like her contempt for the idea of a tuition teacher as a brother, why was I feeling embarrassment about having a driver as a brother-in-law?

That walk home made me realize that I cherished my position in the world. I was a teacher. I saw myself as a professional. The rest of the entourage wherever I went were servants. They were the Rajus who were dispensable and replaceable. I was not.

And what made a driver not-a-professional? He was licensed to drive, wasn't he? And his work was as important as mine. No, perhaps more important. If I did not do my job, a child might fail a test or an examination. This might be bad for his morale, but the kid would bounce back.

If Armaan lost his concentration or mistimed something, people would die.

Only, this did not convince me. Because this argument had not convinced the world. We might teach our children the dignity of labour as a concept, but we would never ask them to clean the toilet bowl. That's the job of the jamadarni. Her work may be important, it may even be vital to our health, but she is not paid as if it were. And she is not treated with respect. Children know this and recognize the dignity of labour as another one of the myriad moral hypocrisies we teach them.

So my problem with Armaan as my brother-in-law was not so much that he was a driver as how the world looks at drivers.

Or so I told myself.

My mother refused to go to their house. And she announced that Anita would not go either.

'Are you sure?' I asked.

Anita looked a bit peeved. She wanted to go and see what this mohalla was like. She wanted to see where Radhika had ended up. I thought it might even be good for her to see, but Mummy was determined. I shrugged and went.

The boys were there, hanging around, but without the air of watchful tension they had had last night. I recognized this only in hindsight.

Three floors up. One-room-kitchen. A great noise from the room which collapsed into an even more deafening silence when I appeared at the door. More people than seemed possible. More furniture than seemed probable. Everything attached to something else so it could be rolled up, put away, hooked to the wall. And in the middle of it all, Imraan, who seemed like a nice chap, the kind you see by the dozen on trains and buses, going to work, holding down a job, eloping with someone else's sister. He did not have any of Armaan's good looks or charm, but he seemed dependable, the kind who would always have some money in the bank and a Plan B in his head.

There was a thin old lady in an armchair, wrapped in a series of blankets that gave her frail body some heft. Her eyes were closed and her toothless mouth moved in silent prayer. She opened them when I came in and I caught a flash of real intelligence. She scanned me from head to foot, decided that I was no threat and shrugged expressively, as if to say: 'I have no part in all this.' Then she closed her eyes again.

Imraan broke the odd silence.

'I am sorry about all this,' he said. 'I tried to tell her.'

She was sitting on the floor.

'Radhika?' I said.

'Meherunissa.' Imraan corrected me. 'Her name is now Meherunissa.'

I shrugged. 'Are you happy?' I asked.

She looked up at me and, suddenly, she smiled and I was dazzled. She was happy. For now, at least.

'Where will you live?'

'It is all fixed,' said Imraan. 'I am going to Riyadh. She will follow…'

'Why can't you take her?'

He looked a bit embarrassed. I looked hard to see if this were a fit of coyness.

'I don't have money for two tickets. Otherwise, my employers prefer married men and they want the wife to come too.'

I took out my cheque book. I had carried it with me.

'My sister will leave with you,' I said and wrote out a cheque for what I thought would be a fair amount.

I felt rather grand until I caught Armaan's cynical eyes on me. In retrospect, I wonder if he had managed this. At that time, I didn't know him at all and so I only thought he could see that I was happy to have got away lightly.

Radhika did not leave immediately, of course. She left a month later. During that month, she tried to visit us on two separate occasions, but she came in a burkha and was turned away at the door. Sethi Mausi took her in on one occasion, gave her tea and no doubt plied her with questions. And so, for a while, Sethi Mausi was added to the list of personae non grata at our home.

Meanwhile, my sex life and my love life continued unabated. I told neither Rewa nor Aparna about the events at home. I don't know why. But I should have known that the truth would out.

A month or so after Radhika left for Riyadh, I was with Rewa. She had spent half an hour with her nose buried in my pubic hair; she had become an expert at oral sex, after the usual pleas and pretence of nausea. (I had not yet trained her to swallow—she said that she could not because she was a vegetarian, but I had the feeling that she might overcome that barrier as well.) And then I had taken her 'against her will', biting her neck, slapping her sides, riding her like a horse until both of us were covered in sweat.

I disengaged and went off to have a shower. There is nothing as wonderful as a post-coital shower with someone else's imported soaps and gels with which you can be lavish.

When I came out, Rewa asked if I would like a cup of tea. I marvelled at her ability to turn from whore and sex toy to South Bombay hausfrau in the time it took for me to wash.

I was feeling at peace with the world and unusually magnanimous. 'Sure,' I said.

'So yoo-er sister is marrying to Armaan brother?' she said as she served me a syrup of milk and cardamom and sugar, lightly flavoured with tea.

'Who told you?' I was so shocked that I did not even bother to try and correct her.

Of course, I already knew. Armaan had told her.

He had needed money for the wedding, Rewa said. They had given him a lakh.

I gasped.

'But kharcha must be from your side also?' she said, her eyes glittering.

I thought about the ticket to Riyadh. 'Yes.'

'And they did kharcha?' she asked.

Some instinct for survival warned me. 'Yes,' I said. 'Inter-caste case, no?'

The glitter died.

I looked for Armaan when I went down to the lobby. He was not there, but on the next occasion that I was teaching Aniruddh, I found him downstairs.

'Kamaaya?' I asked. 'Bhai ke shaadi pe?'

He laughed and threw away his cigarette. Again, I was struck by something, a resemblance...

'Ek do baar hi chance milte hai aise,' he said. And then he said, 'Milke kha sakte hai, Teacher Saahab.'

'Matlab?' I asked.

'Plan hai. Sunoge?'

I almost laughed in his face, and then I realized that he was serious.

'Okay,' I said. 'Bataa.'

'Aise nahin, Teacher Saahab. Baithenge. Kahin baithenge aur main sunaoonga.'

My heart sank. Baithenge is almost always code for: 'Let us drink a lot of alcohol and I will tell you about something silly I want to do that requires you to believe in my business acumen and give me some of your money.'

I almost forgot about it for the rest of the week. Then Armaan cornered me on Saturday. He wanted to meet me. When? I suggested that we meet on Sunday. But where?

'Leave that to me,' he said.

I did and was surprised. It was a three-star hotel to which he summoned me the next day. He looked very comfortable, dressed as if he were Imraan-the-engineer instead of Armaan-the-driver. No tight jeans, no ribbed T-shirt. Instead, he was wearing a business shirt and well-tailored trousers. Nothing was on display. He smiled and explained: his brother was the receptionist.

'Another brother?'

'No, no, a cousin brother.'

Then he pointed with his well-shod foot at a suitcase and my heart sank. Surely, this was not…

Armaan laughed. He could see that I was worried it was charas. Or bombs. 'Aisa kuch nahin hai,' he said. 'Open it and see.'

Gingerly, carefully, I opened the suitcase. Inside it, I found a whole bunch of files. Medical files. Lots of medical files. Different names.

'What are these?' I asked.

'Our passport to wealth.' And he outlined his plan.

It was terrifying. And it was simple.

'What do they pay us?' Armaan asked, and from the sound of his voice it seemed as if he had said this to himself again and again. It had the ring of reasoned rhetoric. 'Nothing. And why do they pay us nothing? Because they say they give us when we need. And when do we need? When someone is in hospital. Now someone is not always in hospital.'

I said nothing.

'Now what happens when we say someone is in hospital? They say: "Bring the papers."'

And then I saw the beauty of this thing. The system under which most employees worked was feudal in a new and terrible way. You have a driver. You give him some white clothes to wear. You pay him a pittance. In so doing, you force him to live in a slum. Perhaps he even has another job. When someone falls ill, perhaps because of the kind of living conditions that slums create, you help with that. This 'help' makes you feel magnificent. It makes you sure that you are a good master. It makes you sure that you deserve the loyalty of everyone who has ever served you for a pittance.

'Here are the papers,' Armaan was saying.

'These are all papers that belong to someone. They have names on them. And dates,' I said. 'Won't work.'

He gave me a pitying look. Then he took out a pad. It was an ordinary pad. A writing pad. Only, it said: 'Shanta Polyclinic'.

'This is our mine.'

Slowly it began to dawn on me. 'There is no Shanta Polyclinic.'

'There is no Shanta Polyclinic,' Armaan agreed.

'But there will be on paper,' I said.

'That is where you come in. We need a bank account.'

'A bank account?'

'Yes,' he said. 'They always say: "I will pay the doctor. I will pay the hospital. I will not give you cash." Why do they say that?'

I took this to be rhetorical, but he was waiting for an answer.

'Because they do not trust us?'

'Because they do not trust us,' Armaan repeated. He had a way of doing that. It seemed as if he were agreeing with you, but it also sounded like he was mocking you for even thinking that there might be another answer. 'So now they will trust. Because we can go to them and show the clinic papers. We will copy them out from these files. And we will show them the bills. Which we will make on these pads.'

He looked at me and, suddenly, he turned into another person. He went from being cock of the walk to being a humble driver. Raju.

'Saahab,' he said, picking up one of the files. 'Yeh rahe kaagzaat. Please do not give me one rupee. But please pay these doctors. You can pay by cheque, sir. You can give me a cheque, sir. I don't mind. I don't mind. But please save my family from ruin.'

And then he threw himself at my feet and buried his head in my lap. I reared up and pushed him off. 'Stop it!'

Lying on the carpet, Armaan glittered at me. I could see his rage and his laughter.

'You know what the trick is?' he asked. 'The trick is the bank account. The trick is the papers. They will give. Oh, they will give. And it will go into a bank account. And then it will come out to you and to me.'

I thought it might be time to talk business. 'As they say in Gujarati: "Maara ketla?"' What would I get?

'Idea kiska?' he asked.

I admitted that the idea was his.

'Papers kaun laya?'

I admitted that the papers were his.

'Bank account kaun banayega?'

He was smart. He was now on my side. I would indeed set up the bank account.

'Aur likhega-vikhega kaun?'

I would also be doing the transcription? I didn't think much of that. Perhaps we could get some help with that? Armaan didn't think so. He had clear reasons and he told me what they were.

'One person can keep a secret. So it is said. Two people, can keep it if both benefit from it. That I feel. Three people, and then it is no secret. Unless everyone gets shares, and even then you are not safe. Two people. Two partners. You and me. My idea. Your bank account. My people. Your writing. This is enough.'

And so it was decided that I would set up the bank account, I would do the paperwork and Armaan would work out the details. He explained that he had already told a couple of drivers and cleaners about the possibility of providing them with fake papers. He explained that there were a couple of gamblers who needed money. These were his first targets.

'They must take someone who has died. No one alive.'

'Why not?' I asked.

'Because, then, if someone really falls sick, people will think: "Oh, I did like this, I did like that, I only made them sick, God is punishing me." And then they will go and cry on this one's shoulder, that one's shoulder, and it will all come out.'

It made sense.

I suggested refinements. 'We shall keep a record so no one can come two-three times in one year.'

He thought about that for a bit. He saw the sense of it. He nodded.

'Except if they work with Parsis.'

'Parsis? Because they are mad?'

'Oho, no one is mad-shad when it comes to money, okay? Don't talk like that.'

I was being lectured on political correctness by an eighth-standard-pass driver?

'Don't feel bad, Teacher Saahab. You are my partner now. And you are my saala. And you are the teacher of my children.'

I took this to be a flourish with the wrong tense attached. I thought he meant that I would teach his children. Some hope. And then I realized that he was my brother-in-law and might have a reasonable expectation of some educational help from me. I felt his gaze on me.

'What about Parsi people, then?'

'Because they are having trusts. They don't have to give their own money. They can give money from other people. So we can do them two or three times a year without any problem.'

It was time to talk about money. Armaan sensed this.

'And now for the deal. Thirty per cent will be mine. Ten per cent will be yours. The rest will be theirs,' he said.

I thought about this for a minute.

'No,' I said. 'Twenty per cent will be yours. Twenty per cent will be mine. The rest will be theirs.'

When we had settled on the figures, I suggested a drink. Armaan laughed. 'Teacher Saahab, I am a Mussalman. Na dukkar ka maas, na sharaab ki baas.'

I was rather relieved. I wondered if he could tell.

As we left the room, he said, 'And, Teacher Saahab, you can ask for a loan for your sister ki shaadi. The boss will give you zero interest. Then you put it in fixed deposit for ten per cent interest. You pay him back regularly and make your ten per cent.'

'Is that what you did with your money?' I asked.

He laughed. 'I don't like fixed rates, Teacher Saahab. Mazaa kya hai if you know how much you're going to make?'

'Then what?' I could already smell a deal. Perhaps I could...

'Better you should not know,' he said, and his face closed up.

But I did ask the Jinkses for a loan for my sister's wedding and asked that they cut it from my pay.

I got some letterheads made, and some envelopes. Armaan was all for doing them on a DTP set-up, but I thought we should spend some money and do a good job of it. I got a friend to countersign a current account in the name of Integrated Health Services. The bank clerk who did the paperwork wanted to know more about it, but when I gave him a couple of Gandhis he lost interest and, within the day, I had made my first cash deposit.

When the Jinkses gave me a zero per cent loan for my sister's wedding in cash, it occurred to me that several other families could be similarly tapped. I went to each with the same proposition. I would give them a set of ten post-dated cheques, which they could deposit at regular intervals.

At the end of the week, I had nearly ten lakhs in cash. I deposited these sums in various banks, all in my mother's name. Still slightly in shock over Radhika's wedding, she signed the joint holder forms without asking too many questions.

I was already earning a steady amount from the interest. I wondered if I should lend it out at a higher rate of interest. But Armaan, with whom I had begun to drink a cup of tapri chai every time I went to the Jinkses, said I shouldn't.

Was this the point at which I realized how much I had come to rely on his worldly wisdom? Not that I asked him for advice. I just mentioned the possibility of lending out the money to him, in passing, and waited for his reaction. He was unequivocal.

'Teacher Saahab, you will not be able to do that business.'

'Why not?' I bristled.

'Because you cannot see a woman cry.'

'You can?'

'Forget me. This talk is not about me. This talk is about you. Suppose there is one child who is holding a gold chain and you have to take that gold chain and the child starts crying and says it is his grandmother's aakhri nishaani. What will you do then?'

I shrugged.

'You will not be able to take it. Why will you not be able to take it? Because you do not know that the child has been trained to say like that. Will you be able to take the child the next time and hold him upside down and shake him until he screams?' he asked.

'Why would anyone do that?'

'Why? Because everyone knows that one time you may get away with that. But next time, they have decided, we will take the chain from the child, whether he cries or screams or does hullagulla. The man says: "Where is that aakhri nishaani, maaderchod?" You don't say anything. You can't say anything. Your mother has made you put the chain in your mouth. Then the man picks you up and shakes you and your mouth opens and he tries to keep it open, so you bite him. He screams and lets you go, but there is another man with him. That man steps up and grabs you and holds you upside down and shakes you until you can't breathe, so you scream and the chain falls out and he drops you on the floor. You fall on your head when the man drops you and your ears ring, but when they have left your mother slaps you and she is weeping because her gold chain is gone. There is nothing left now, understand? Nothing left.'

Armaan was looking straight at the ground. He spat out the tea as if it was bitter. I felt cold too, as if I had looked into someone else's head. Then he shrugged, gave me a half-smile and took out a slip of paper. There was a name on it.

'Good for one lakh at least,' he said. 'Get the papers ready, Teacher Saahab.'

'How does he know one lakh?'

'Because he is the guy who updates the bank books as well, Teacher Saahab. He knows who has hidden what and where.'

This sounded reasonable and that evening we met at the hotel, in another room. Armaan startled me with a rubber stamp that said Shanta Polyclinic. He also helped with the writing, although I didn't think he should.

'Why not?' He seemed offended.

'Your letters. They're illiterate.' His handwriting looked like that of a four-year-old girl—all fat, round letters.

'How can letters be illiterate? Only people can be illiterate.'

I shrugged. I opened a couple of files. 'See?' I pointed to the squiggles.

'What do I see? That people write badly? Doctors' handwriting…'

'Haan. Doctors' handwriting. They are busy. They write fast. They don't take time like that. They don't make letters like that.'

He took a couple of files and began to look through them.

'Sahi re,' he said, and his voice was different now—it was that of a child accepting a truth that should have been self-evident. For the first time, he sounded almost respectful.

Armaan turned the sheets he had written over and began to try and write as a doctor might. Only, he wrote too large. I pointed this out.

'What a world we live in,' he said. 'To look like I am a doctor, I must write like a farmer.' And he grinned at me.

I was struck once again at how handsome he was, how his smile brightened his face…and something else, something I couldn't catch. It was as if I had seen him somewhere else.

Later, when we had finished a nice pile of papers, he stretched and said, 'Ek maarenge?'

'I thought you didn't drink?'

'I don't,' he said, and took out a beautiful cigarette case. It was silver, I could tell, and he had had the good sense to let it tarnish. He took out a cigarette with care, as if it were a rare flower whose bloom might be spoilt by too much careless touching. He lit it and a sweet odour came wafting across to me.

'What is it?' I asked as he handed it to me.

He shrugged. 'If you want it, take it. Don't put names on everything.'

I took a long drag and felt precisely nothing. Armaan kicked off his shoes and went to lie down on the bed. I took another drag, then walked over to the bed to hand him the cigarette. The world was very quiet. It was quite quiet. You could quit while it was quite quiet. Qui could quit while Keith is quite quiet?

'I am high,' I thought. But it was nice.

Armaan beckoned from the bed. He had taken off his shirt and was wearing a ribbed banian. I took off my shoes slowly, as if my actions were all premeditated and needed to be scrutinized thoroughly, and then went and lay down beside him. We passed the joint between us.

'How come you're not married?' I asked.

Armaan shrugged. It seemed to be his favourite means of communication. 'When your plate is full, you should not get up,' he said.

This made a great deal of sense to me then, but it seemed completely meaningless about an hour later. I was eating my third chocolate bar when Aparna showed up. We kissed and she licked some of the chocolate off my tongue. I thought it was intensely erotic and gave her a bite of chocolate to eat. Then I made her open her mouth and took it back. We passed it back and forth between us and she giggled.

'If someone had told me I'd be doing this with a guy, I'd have been shocked,' she said.

'Love is funny like that,' I said, and then I could have bitten off my tongue.

That word. That forbidden word. And I had gone and dropped it into the middle of the conversation.

But it was too late. Aparna had heard and she was pushing her body against mine and kissing my face and generally behaving like she or I or both of us had won the Nobel Prize for something or the other.

'I love you too,' she said.

'I can get her into bed right now,' I thought. 'I can take her on my bike to one of those pay-by-the-hour hotels and I can have sex with her right now.' But I was strangely reluctant. Perhaps it was because I liked Aparna and did not want to cheat her. Perhaps it was because I was getting as much sex as I needed and so didn't have to push it. I thought I might test it out, however, and so I slowly ran a finger along the neckline of her kurta. There was no protest. I ran it back even as I kissed her ear and licked behind it, and then let my finger trace the soft, slow swell of her breasts. I was still moving as if through cotton wool, but the feelings were quite exquisite, as if strained and sieved and passed on to me pure, refined. I wanted to weep at how lovely the feeling was. When my finger became constrained by cloth, I decided against further moves. There was no point in clumsiness. There was no point in a lack of beauty.

'It should be beautiful between us,' I said.

Aparna laughed with delight, a tinkling sound in the middle of the traffic, in the rough rasp of retreating tide along the shoreline.

I should have felt bad about all this. I see that now. I should have known that Aparna would not forgive my behaviour, but those two parts of my world were completely separate.

Aparna represented my social life; Rewa was part of my

professional world. That I was having sex with her didn't seem very different from teaching her children. I know it sounds bizarre, but that's what it was.

Rewa and I had now worked out a fairly good relationship. She would give me money, but it was always money I needed. I would point out that my bike needed servicing and that it would cost two thousand rupees. I would say that my sister needed new clothes and that it would cost three thousand rupees. I tried to match the money to the level of service.

But the truth was that I had no heart for it. Rewa wanted to be treated badly; however, there was a limit to what I could do. I thought it would be enough to get her to worship my feet or to leave my dick inside her mouth for ten or fifteen minutes, but it seemed as if I needed to be upping the ante each time we went at it. I tried some research and pushed her head into the toilet bowl and flushed, which made her orgasm intense but almost lost me my erection because when she bucked under me drops of water splashed all over my torso—I did not know whether this was her sweat or the water from the commode.

I also began to see why prostitution was not really a fun profession as I had always thought. When I was growing up, I had always fantasized about being paid to fuck. I thought it would be really cool to be, say, sitting in a bar, and then this amazing woman comes up to you and offers you money to bring her off. I did not have any of the details worked out. In college, we were always being told that you had to stand at the Wilson College bus stop with a handkerchief peeking out of a pocket, and this was a signal to the sexy aunties of the area whose husbands were too busy to service them. I was very tempted to do this, but it sounded like some kind of fantasy. I didn't know how women would be able to spot a handkerchief and check out a young man and decide on whether to sleep with him in the time it took for her to pass a bus stop. And did women really choose that way? Whatever the truth of that rumour, I had found the idea of someone wanting me enough to pay for it incredibly sexy. Now, when I thought of it, I did not feel the usual physical memory of sexual excitement, the faint fluffing out of my penis, the trickle of delight inside my head.

And, truth be told, I wasn't particularly concerned about the money that Rewa gave me. Armaan and I were making a steady income from our side business. He seemed to have a steady supply of people and he seemed to know what we would get.

'Ishwar will ask for fifty thousand, they will give him forty,' he would say.

'Why?'

'He is a relatively new banda in their household, but he is chikna.'

'You mean someone is having a chakkar with him?'

I did not know why I spoke in a different way with him, but I did. Did I do it to make him comfortable? Or to change who I was?

'Arre, everything is not sex. They are an old couple, both are finished with their vaasanas. But old people also like young people to be around. They have an old man in the kitchen who has been there fifty years, his name is Manoj Kaka. They just gave him one lakh to rebuild his kholi in the village. And all this even after he has been named in their will.'

'How do you know all this?'

'The old one was boasting. See, Manoj Kaka is jealous. He does not like that "Munna" gets to do this, gets to do that. He can see that when "Munna" comes into the room the oldies are smiling. He wonders whether they will change their will. So he wants to take it out now only. There was no problem with the kholi in the village, but he managed to take out one lakh, so he told Ishwar. He is an old fool, because now Ishwar is ready to take out also.'

One day, I saw the two of them together and joined them for a cup of tea.

'I am telling him, Teacher Saahab, to listen to me. You tell him.'

I thought about this for a moment. Would I listen to Armaan? I would.

'If it is about duniyadaari,' I said to Ishwar, who seemed to be paying attention to me as if he were willing to follow my advice to the grave, 'you cannot find a better guide.'

Ishwar said, 'Thank you, sir. I will listen to him, sir. Sir, with you as my guide...'

'Oy,' said Armaan, his voice abrasive. 'He is not a pigeon for you to pluck.'

And it dawned on me that Ishwar had been using his stock-in-trade: he had been showing himself as the young and humble man who is willing to listen.

'So what is this about?' I asked as I lit a cigarette and took my first sip of tea.

'What to say? Money has come into the hand and he is saying give it back.' Ishwar sighed.

I raised an eyebrow.

'The oldies gave only thirty thousand rupees,' said Armaan.

I continued to look puzzled. Armaan sighed.

'I am telling this fool to return the money and say nothing.'

I shrugged my shoulders and looked at Ishwar. 'Do as he tells you.'

'If I do not take one lakh out of these people,' said Armaan, 'I will give you thirty thousand rupees of my own money.'

He then outlined the plan. Ishwar was to go back and give the money to his oldies without a word. He was to say: 'I asked you for money and you gave it to me. I am grateful for your help. Here is your money back.'

'Can you say that much without smiling your jalebi smile?' asked Armaan.

'Arre, I am giving money back. I am sending Goddess

Lakshmi home. What source of happiness will make me smile?'

'I will tell you what to say and you say it. I will tell you what to do and you do it,' said Armaan. 'Just follow my orders and you will be washing your backside into gold vessels.'

I thought this rather crude, but the sentiment seemed to appeal to Ishwar. In due course, we made our cut of the money. It was forty thousand—the one lakh had come through.

'How?' I asked Armaan as we lay in bed, smoking. It had become a habit now, this Sunday afternoon marijuana session. I would get the writing done in an hour or so. Armaan did the nursing notes because they could have somewhat girly-curly handwriting. We worked on a couple of sets of medical notes a week and then we relaxed.

'Simple. He goes and returns the money. They are shocked. They say: "Don't you need it?" He says: "My brother is sick. He is dying. Of course I need it. But I do not want it this way." They say: "Are you mad?" He says: "You must be having problems with money. You are like my parents. If you cannot give me the full money, it must be because you do not have it yourselves. I cannot take money from my parents if it hurts them." They say: "No, take it, no take it." But luckily he has the sense to follow my instructions. When they are getting angry, he falls at their feet and says that he actually needs one lakh, but he could not ask them for it because they have just given so much money to Manoj Kaka and how could he ask for one lakh after that and even with fifty thousand nothing will happen and so on and so on. So, the next day, they got the money for him.'

I laughed. 'I feel sorry for them.'

'You do?' Armaan looked at me with something like curiosity. 'Why?'

'They're so easy to con,' I said, but there was something frightening in his eyes.

'Easy to con? Do you know who is easy to con? Ishwar. I can take his panties away from him tomorrow and he won't know.'

'I think you could take mine and I wouldn't know,' I said, trying to calm him down.

'No, I can't do that. You have education. You can take that education and go out into the market and ask for your price. What does Ishwar have? He has his hands. When the old man shits in his bed, you know who cleans it up? Ishwar. When the old woman dribbles on her dried-up tits, you know who cleans it up? Ishwar. When they get up in the middle of the night, Ishwar gets up in the middle of the night. When they are sitting at the table, they tell him bring this, bring that, then they laugh when he does not know what this or that is. Arre, he is a boy from a small pahari village. Where has he seen fork-knife-dish-spoon? But they think he must know. He must know because Manoj Kaka knows. Manoj Kaka has been there how long? Twenty-five, thirty years. He has had time. He knows this goes here, that goes there. He wants his nephew to work in that house, but his nephew is a drunkard, he will not do this, he will not do that. He gets drunk and one day he starts shouting at the old lady when she makes a mess. He gets sacked and who comes in? Ishwar. When the nephew was there, Manoj Kaka made sure the oldies gave him five thousand rupees. When Ishwar came, how much did he get? He gets two thousand rupees. Now tell me, who is easy to con? Is it the buddha-buddhi or is Ishwar?'

'I see what you mean,' I said.

'You cannot see what it means,' Armaan said. 'Because I look into your eyes and I see innocence.'

I felt a flicker of annoyance. This was perhaps going too far.

'One day,' said Armaan, 'I will tell you my story.'

'Why one day?' I asked. 'Tell now.'

'Your girl is not waiting for you?'

I didn't even ask how he knew I had a girl. The driver network was alive and well.

'She's not in town.' It was true. Aparna was in Coorg, on a field trip, with her class.

'My father wanted to do business, but he was an innocent,' Armaan began. 'He helped people and he thought people would help him in his hour of need. Because that is what you need when you start a business. You need people to help you.'

This was familiar territory. I had heard this story a dozen times before from a dozen different sons. Dad was never a failure. He was never just a bad businessman. He had never over-estimated the demand for his product. He had never got his supply chain wrong. He was just a good man who was treated badly. This made it easy to handle. This made your father's failure into a decent story. For a moment, Armaan's mask slipped. He was not the sophisticated worldly-wise man who knew how to milk the system. He was just another boy whose father had let him down.

'When people came to him, he helped them. And then he found he had no money left.'

And so Armaan's father borrowed one lakh rupees, back in the day when one lakh rupees meant something. That too went to the poor and the needy. Or so Armaan said.

'Do you know how you can repay money like that?' Armaan asked.

I shrugged.

'There aren't those many ways,' he said. 'You can sell a kidney, but you rarely get enough money. My cousin brother did that. The dalaal told him that he would get one lakh rupees, cash. But on the morning of the operation, he brought only forty thousand.'

'Why did he agree to go through with it?'

'Because his father grabbed the forty thousand and ran. Then there was no discussion. He went under the knife. When he came out on the other side, they said: "Your kidney was not as good as it should have been. It was a bit this, it was a bit that." So many words, so many descriptions. How can one say anything? He said he would go to the police, but they laughed in his face. In this country, there is no police for Muslims, there is only police against Muslims.'

I didn't know what to say to that. Again, the difference in who he was and who I was yawned between us. I did not think of the police as my friends either, but I did not think that they were actively against me.

'The kidney thing? It's no good. Another person went. Rameshwar, his name was. He was from the bhaiyas down the road. He was picked up at the free dinner thing. You know the place on Cadell Road, where cars stop and they give hundred rupees or thousand rupees or whatever it is, and so many people get fed? One day a car stopped and they took three people away for testing. Gave them lots of food. Took their blood. Took samples. All sent back with hundred-hundred rupees in the pocket. Next day, again. And again. Finally, Rameshwar's turn. He was all right. His kidney was all right too. They took his kidney, gave him fifty thousand rupees. But the patient died anyway and someone got mad. I don't know who it was, but he came in the night, with the kidney in his hand, and he beat Rameshwar to death and stuffed his own kidney into his mouth.'

I did not know whether to believe this story or not. It seemed to have the ring of truth in it, but it also seemed like something out of the tabloids.

'Kidney is one way. Or you can take a bag somewhere. One bag, five thousand rupees. The only problem is: if you get caught, you go to jail. Or worse. One of my friends took a bag. He got on the train and put it on the rack. Then he was standing at the window. Then someone came and put a big bag right on top and my friend's bag burst. The powder began to trickle out. He panicked and jumped from the running train. That's it. Finished. There only. Another one, I heard about this, he was caught and the police did the worst thing to him. They took his bag and shared it among themselves and told him to go home. He knew what would happen if he went home without the bag. He begged them to put him behind bars, but they refused. So he threw himself into the sea. Finished.'

The nasha was coming down slowly. I was re-entering the real world. Armaan took another joint out of his box and lit it. He did not offer it to me, so I took it from his fingers.

'Take it, take it. How else to live in this world?' he asked.

I heard the sound of an invisible Bollywood dialogue writer in his voice, but with every puff of the grass I felt a deeper and deeper sympathy for him. I reached across and patted him on the shoulder. He sighed and nuzzled into my palm. I felt a little strange about this, but once again I was lifted on the wave of sympathetic understanding and let it go, let it go.

'So, do you know what I did, Teacher Saahab? I came to this very hotel, where there was a man who was taking children to the Gulf. For the camel races. It was not hard work, someone had told me. You would be tied to a camel and you had to just stay on and they would pay you and feed you and clothe you and everything.'

I had read about this. What was it? A slave ring, yes, in which Indian children were sold to Dubai and they rode camels. Some of them were bought from beggar parents. And they killed each other, didn't they? Or they became addicts. Or they were killed. Either way, it was something very terrible.

'This man was the dealer, so I came with my cousin, the same one who works in this hotel now. I told this man our story and he said: "Okay, I will buy you. Take off your clothes." My cousin said: "No, this is not why we have come." And the man said: "This is nothing like that, you donkey. This is to take his weight." I did not know what weight had to do with it, but I took off my shirt-pant. I was wearing shorts underneath my pant. Where we had underwear those days? He said: "That also must go." I thought about Ammi and I took that off also.'

'How old were you?'

'Fourteen,' he said. 'Everything was there,' he added and pointed to his crotch. 'And here,' he pointed to his underarms. 'Nothing here yet,' he said, pointing to his chest. 'Or here,' he said pointing to his head and laughing. It was not a pleasant sound.

'What did he do?'

'He? He did nothing. He was examining the maal. There was maal. He asked me: "It stands?" I said yes. He asked me: "It spits?" I didn't even know what he meant, but I said yes. He said: "Do you want to earn lots of money?" I said: "Who does not want to earn lots of money?" He took my maal in his hand and twisted hard. I screamed. "Don't show me how smart you are. Just answer my questions. If you want lots of money, I can show you how to make lots of money. But you will have to do what I tell you.'"

Armaan told me a sordid tale—the kind you hear every day in this city, he said. I had never heard anything like it. No one I knew had ever been asked to massage strange men who came into the city and asked for boys to be sent to their rooms. No one I knew had ever exchanged his anal virginity for money and a gold coin. (This he wore on a chain around his neck; the chain was a gift from another of his clients, a Dubai-return, he said.)

I had no way to respond to any of this. I felt sorry for Armaan and I felt sorry for Radhika or Meherunissa or whatever she called herself now. She had married into a family that had been forced into sex work.

I felt a little sick now.

'Bye, Teacher Saahab,' said Armaan, and his voice was sleepy, as if he were drifting away. 'Next time, if you don't want to know, you shouldn't ask.'

This was unanswerable because one always wanted to know when one did ask; it was only when the answer fell into the realm of the unacceptable that one wished one hadn't asked. However, curiosity has always been my besetting sin and I know that I must live with the consequences.

I thought about saying some of this to Armaan. When I looked back at him, he had closed his eyes and seemed to be falling asleep. And once again there was something in his face that looked familiar.

I do not know when I realized that Armaan had become something of a friend. I did not have many, as the life of a tuition teacher tends to be somewhat solitary. I did know a few other teachers who passed on students they could not or did not want to handle to me, in return for a commission; I reciprocated but did not expect to be paid. I was, after all, the new kid on the block. Once in a while, a teacher might slip me a five-hundred rupee note for a particularly good contact, but I didn't bother much with all that. I now had three sources of income, all of them pretty good.

It did not occur to me that I could up the take from Stream 2. After all, how many times can a man perform? I was having sex about once a week with Rewa, and that seemed adequate. I did not think to ask whether she wanted me to come more often. I wasn't even sure I wanted to go more often. Of course, there were other women in the world, but even when I did think about it I could see that there were many dangers involved. There were times when I had felt, in the past, that a pupil's mother might be flirting a little with me, but I could never be sure. There are many things women want from men and sex isn't always on the list. What if I started something, suggested something, and things went wrong? The woman might scream blue murder, she might let her friends know… There was no saying where it all would end. Which woman would hire a lecher for her teenage daughter? Or even for her son? After all, it would be suspected that she was hiring him for herself.

And then, one day, I was having a bath in Rewa's bathroom and trying to feel clean again after I had spit in her face and made her clean my shoes with her tongue. Rewa was nattering on outside the door about the price of vegetables. I suddenly thought: 'I feel like a husband.' In fact, we had got into something of a rhythm, with her making me a cup of tea and a sandwich before I left for the next lot of tuitions.

'This lady,' she said when she set down a plate of miniature cheese toasties and chai, 'she toh told to me…'

'She told me,' I said.

'She told to you?' Rewa's pretty brow furrowed.

'No, I meant you have to say "She told me", not "She told to me". You can say "She said to me", or you can say "She told me".'

'Why?' she asked. 'Why like that?'

I shrugged.

'This is very funny language,' she said. 'So she said me, "Do you know anyone who will teach English?" I said, "You also want English teacher?" And then I am thinking, "Ofho, what I have said?"'

I thought it pretty funny too. But then it occurred to me that perhaps this lady was indeed looking for someone to teach her English.

'So who is she?'

'I will not tell,' said Rewa. I had to twist her arm—and I am sorry to say that I mean this literally—before she would give me the number. I called almost immediately and was greeted by a soft voice. Her name was Anukriti, her friends called her Anu.

We made a date, sorry, an appointment, for the next week, on Wednesday. That was the day I usually met Rewa. I calculated that I could manage a quickie and then rush over to the new English student.

When I rang Rewa's bell, she opened the door only a crack. 'What are you doing here?' she asked in Hindi.

'Class time,' I said.

'Class-flass,' she said. 'You have another student, go there.'

Then she slammed the door. In the courtyard of the building, I met Armaan. He had a quiet smile for me, an understanding smile.

'Memsahib is now learning aerobics,' he said.

I looked at him carefully.

'Memsahib likes to learn many things,' he said, and there was now a glint in his eyes.

'I have to go,' I said.

'Haan, haan,' he said. 'Run along now.'

I wanted to hit him. I had to remind myself that I did not love Rewa and that I had also been tiring of the mechanical nature of our exchanges. How was one supposed to do something one did not want to? Of course, she was a beautiful woman, and as soon as I saw those pink-berry nipples, set back in her plump breasts, I was ready for anything. I wondered if the aerobics instructor would discover her needs as I had. I wondered if he would be shocked or if he would be delighted. I wondered if he was like Armaan, someone from a slum or a tenement. I even began to wonder if I were getting a little fat. I reached under my shirt and pinched at my side. A roll of new fat greeted me cheerfully. 'Yes, it's your new love handles, sir,' it said. 'Why don't you drive that bike a little more? Why don't you drink some more tea, eat some more cheese sandwiches, take another toke and then gobble three chocolate bars?'

I promised myself that I would go to the gym more often and rang the bell of my new student's house. If a servant opened the door…

It was not a servant. But the woman who opened the door seemed to be of a certain age. To put it plainly, I had not expected someone who was clearly on the wrong side of forty and only a few birthdays short of fifty. She was fighting this gamely. Her hair was dark red and black in almost equal measure and her skin was so well cared for that it had the look of ancient parchment. I decided as I followed her into the living room that I was going to stick to English. No extras.

But, within a few minutes, it was clear that she was looking for some extras. When I sat down on the sofa, she sat next to me instead of across from me. She let her knee brush mine as she leant across the teapoy to pour me some coffee. She explained that her children had left home and that she was bored. (She said 'borudd'.) She wanted to acquire some polish. (She said 'poll-is'.)

I grew tired of this after a while. I reached out and drew one of her dark-red locks into my fingers and stroked it.

'You must learn to love English,' I said.

'I have heard you are a very good teacher,' she replied.

So Rewa had been talking.

'Rewa and I are like that,' she said, and showed me two fingers twined.

I took her hand and gently pulled her fingers apart. 'Now you and I will be like that,' I said, and led her into the bedroom. It was ready for us, the bed turned down and waiting, the incense burning, the lights turned low. So what if Anukriti-call-me-Anu was in her late forties? She was wearing black lace underwear and her body was fit and beautifully ready. Where Rewa had a full pubic bush, Anu was Brazilian-waxed. Her inner thighs were like steel whereas Rewa's were intensely feminine and fit together like rabbits that cohabit.

We had vanilla sex the first time, me on top, she underneath. She seemed very, very ready and intense about enjoying herself. This was useful, even if there was a hint of desperation in it. Whatever I did, she seemed ready to orgasm. I had only to lick her prickly armpit as I had learnt to or nibble my way down her spine and she would be writhing and wriggling like a fish out of water.

But she was also a slave to novelty. Rather, she wanted me to be a slave to her desire for novelty. I could not do anything twice.

'You did that last time,' she said once when I was licking the back of her knees.

'You did that last time to last time,' she said when I slid the blade of my hand between her buttocks. Since I had got this new move from the video parlour, I was annoyed. She was obviously lying. She didn't like it, so she wanted me to feel I wasn't doing what I should.

'Do you keep score?' I asked.

'No, but I pay,' she said.

With Anu, it was clear where we stood and how we were going to go forward. On the first day, she pointed to an envelope she had placed on the dining table and said with a half-smile: 'If this is not enough, then it is not enough. I will not give more, but I will not give less.'

When I went down in the lift, the packet was burning a hole in my pocket. It seemed rather slim, but when I opened it there were ten five-hundred-rupee notes inside. That made me feel a little better, but there was something about Anu's age and her clinical detachment about the whole thing that made me feel sordid.

So I did what I always did in those days when I was feeling a little down. I went off to the bank and checked my balance. It was healthy beyond my belief. I wondered if I should risk playing the stock market, but after a little consideration decided against it. I didn't know what I was doing and I might lose all that I had gained with the work of my hands and my head and my cock. Instead, I decided that it was time to put down a deposit on a home in some far-flung suburb. Even if I never did live there, it could be an investment for the future.

In the course of a week, it was all over.

I went to the Jinkses' home to teach the young ones and was met by Mr Jinks himself. He was wearing a lungi and nothing else. One immense thigh was visible again.

'From tomorrow, you do not come,' he said.

I must have looked startled.

'Yes, you have to give us money. That is maaf. Gurudakshina from my children.'

'May I say goodbye to them?'

I don't even know why I asked. I had no special affection for the two brats and it was likely that Mr Jinks also knew this. But he shrugged. I went and opened the door to their bedroom. They were both in bed, their eyes closed and, suddenly, I knew why Armaan had seemed familiar. Masked in baby fat, softened by youth, here was his face, reflected twice over. It was such a shock that I turned in amazement and said, 'Armaan...' and then tailed off because I did not know how to complete the sentence.

The effect on Mr Jinks was electric. He leapt up from his sofa, galloped across the polished white marble floor and slammed shut the door of the children's bedroom.

'He is also not here. He has gone.'

'Gone?'

'Don't you know? Gone to Dubai.'

I had not seen Armaan for a few days—but gone to Dubai? Why hadn't he told me? Why hadn't he told me about the children?

'These people go to Dubai like you people go to native place,' said Mr Jinks, urging me to the door.

'My fees?' I said.

'You are a full hubshi. You have taken loan. I am saying that is maaf. Still you want your fees?'

I felt a bit foolish.

'Now you go,' said Mr Jinks. 'And don't come. What-what people.'

The door closed in my face.

Later, in the evening, I went to Armaan's house. I had never been there after the first time and Armaan had not seemed to think it necessary either. He was content to meet in the hotel room down the road. The one-room home seemed to have the same number of people as when I had come the last time. The old lady seemed to be in the same position, with the same number of quilts, making the same movements with her mouth as she said her prayers.

'Maaji,' I said.

She opened her eyes.

'Chale gaye,' she said. 'Sab chale gaye.'

And she closed her eyes.

Then she opened her eyes again and said, 'Tum bhi jaao Dubai. Tum jaiso ke liye best place.'

I didn't know what she meant, but I didn't want to find out. I had the curious feeling these days of being made of glass. Anyone who wanted to could look into me and discover my fell purposes.

That night, I woke up from a terrible dream in which I had written everything down and everyone had read what I had written.

The only way to deal with a terrible dream is to make it a reality.

I am making this a reality.

I am writing this in an airport.

I am on my way to Dubai.

What did I do? How come I acted on the advice of an illiterate old woman who pimped out her own son?

You have to understand that I have learnt my lesson. Wisdom does not always come with learning. It comes when life smacks you in the face.

I was already feeling the loss of Armaan. Without him and his contacts in the servant community, there was no more money to be made out of Shanta Polyclinic. I didn't even want to. Without Armaan, I felt exposed, vulnerable. Ishwar had tried to approach me once, but I was brusque. I had nothing to do with anything like that, I told him.

And then it all came apart.

I went to see Anukriti, once again certain that I wanted to break it off.

The house was looking different.

'Spring cleaning?' I asked, wandering around the room. I stopped at a case of fine watches that had been moved around. 'Nice watches.'

'They are my husband's collection,' she said. 'Come and sit down.'

There was tea and cake.

'Nice cake,' I said.

'Eggless,' she said. Like I cared. And then she added: 'It is my birthday today.' Naturally, she said 'birday'.

'Happy birthday.'

'Mere liye gift?' she asked.

I took her hand and put it on my crotch. 'This is your gift.'

As far as cheesy lines go, this had to be one of the worst. As far as gifts go, it might have been much better if I had had an erection, but I couldn't get it up until I saw her body. Her face was too much of a mask, too smooth and too odd for nature. But once I had flipped her over and was biting the back of her neck as I took her doggie-style, this did not matter. What mattered was that I was now buried inside a beautiful body. But today, she insisted on doing it face-to-face.

We were sitting in bed and she was rising and falling on my lap when the door opened and a whole bunch of women rushed into the room, shouting: 'Surprise, surprise! Happy birthday!'

At the head of the bunch, bearing a cake, was Aparna. Behind her was Rewa.

My cock shrivelled.

Anu buried her face first in my shoulder and then, as I shot out of bed, into her pillow.

The women shrieked. I thought I saw Rewa hurry out of the room. I could not swear to it, but she seemed to be smiling.

Aparna said, 'Ma…?'

Then she dropped the cake and turned and fled.

'Please excuse us,' I said, trying for as much dignity as you can when you're naked and a whole bunch of women are ooh-ing and aah-ing around you. They were gone when I had dressed.

I tried to say something to Anukriti, but she was sobbing passionately, her head still buried in the pillow.

Do I regret taking the envelope I found in the usual place? Perhaps. But I couldn't help it. Rewa was not the only face in the crowd that I had recognized. There were other women there too, women whose children I was teaching. They would have to sack me just in order to keep their reputations safe.

Word would spread.

Soon, I was going to be without a job, without any means of earning. I simply telephoned each one of the parents and explained that I would no longer be able to teach their children. I suggested other teachers and did not even bother to check whether they had taken them or not.

I lay in bed at home, trying not to listen to my mother moaning and groaning about the state in which Sethi Mausi had left the steel plates she had lent her last week. My life was finished, and all my mother could bother about was Sethi Mausi's savage use of steel wool. A line came back to me from my college English literature class. 'About suffering they were never wrong, the Old Masters.' The lecturer had shown us a slide of the painting he was on about—in one corner a small splash marked the end of Icarus, but planting and sowing and whatnot just went on.

The phone rang. 'Some girl called Aparna,' Mummy came up to the bed and snapped. My heart lifted, but I decided that I could not talk to her.

Two hours later, Aparna called again. This time, I thought, I should take the call. She said, and I could hear the tears in her voice: 'Mom killed herself. Thank you.' Then she hung up.

I tried calling her back, but the call kept ringing out. I dialled again and again. Finally, Aparna picked up the phone.

Her voice was cold and dry. 'If you ever try to contact me again, I will let the police know that you were an accessory.'

I tried to laugh this off, but I kept thinking of that model who had killed herself. Her boyfriend had been dragged to the police station again and again. Maybe he had even appeared in court. I couldn't recall. But as far as I could remember, his crime seemed to have been that they were a couple and she had killed herself.

This could happen to me.

The next morning, I made a down payment on a house in Vasai. I put it in Mummy's name and emptied my bank account.

I tried to get back to the law. I went to the USIS library and tried to work. When I came home, there was a blue envelope from one Meherunnissa Sheikh. It was my sister, of course.

'Armaan bhaiya is working in a hotel as a masseur. He is very busy and is enjoying Dubai too much. He says you should also come here. He says you can stay in his room.'

Within the week, I was buying my ticket. I was going to Dubai. I was going to start again.

There must be children in Dubai who need coaching.

And those children will have mothers.

This time, I will lock the bedroom door.

Coming soon...

CONFESSIONS OF
A CALL CENTRE WORKER

KRIS YONZONE

A small-town boy moves to the big city to get away from a government-job-obsessed family and realize his dreams. He joins a call centre to make money—and finds himself turning into just one of the many unknown nightshift workers of India.

After clearing round after round of interviews with managers and assessors from every ass-monkey department they had, I was finally selected to work for Big Blue as a technical support agent (whatever the fuck that was). The less unfortunate slunk back into whatever holes they crawled out from, to the victor went the spoils. On the bus journey back to my rat hole of a flat, while being assaulted by the unwashed armpits of India, I remember being distinctly happy to have a job with a multinational, even if it was a call centre. It was only later, much later, that I realized that taking calls for a living is frowned upon in India—the funny stares I got from people made me feel like maybe I would be better off shovelling some ripe cow dung.

May 2013